I0677519

ADOPTION

Adoption

by Victoria I. Sullivan

For you did not receive a spirit of slavery to fall back into fear,
but you have received a spirit of adoption. Psalm 8:14.

Pinyon Publishing
MONTROSE, CO

Copyright © 2010 by Victoria I. Sullivan

All rights reserved. Except as permitted under the U.S.
Copyright Act of 1976, no part of this publication may be
reproduced, distributed, or transmitted in any form or by any
means, or stored in a database or retrieval system, without
the prior written permission of the publisher, except for brief
quotations in articles, books, and reviews.

Back Cover Photograph of Victoria I. Sullivan Copyright © 2010
by Diane M. Moore

First Edition: December 2010

Pinyon Publishing
23847 V66 Trail, Montrose, CO 81403
www.pinyon-publishing.com

Library of Congress Control Number: 2010940938
ISBN: 978-1-936671-00-7

ACKNOWLEDGEMENTS

My biggest thanks goes to poet and novelist, Diane M. Moore, for her editing of an early version of the manuscript, and for being a wellspring of encouragement and patience in listening to my ideas. I thank Gary Entsminger at Pinyon Publishing for his faith in the book and his expert editing. And to Susan Elliott for her design artistry.

Early versions benefited from the instruction of science fiction author John DeChancie and fellow writers, Pierre Desilets, Marge Perko, Joanna Bright, Hugo Janke, and Michelle Cross in the Extended Novel Writing Workshop of Writer's Digest. Also, I thank writer and author JoAnn Lordahl for suggestions regarding early drafts and Bill Keller for his insightful impressions of the novel. Others who encouraged me without knowing are too numerous to list, but I thank them for the light of excitement in their eyes when I described the premise of *Adoption*.

Last, but most importantly, I thank creation for the evolution of diploid species and polyploid races within the genus *Eupatorium*, in the plant family Asteraceae. Decades of studying *Eupatorium* inspired this anthropomorphic extension to humans.

To Diane M. Moore
for her undying encouragement

PROLOGUE

I remember when I was born—six years ago. Mommy says it's impossible that I'd remember my birth. Of course, I didn't know the date. Babies don't know dates. But I remember faces and voices. Mommy was smiling and crying at the same time, and I didn't understand what she was saying. But the sound of her voice made me happy.

I was very hungry, and I'm still almost always hungry. It's hard to get enough to eat. She nursed me, but her milk wasn't enough. She brought me to the condo where we live now. I remember a man's face. He looked into my crib but didn't talk or pick me up. He stretched my arms and legs, examined my hands and toes, and turned me over. Then I never saw him again.

My crib became too small, and Mommy moved me to a regular bed. I understood what she was saying, and I replied in Russian. That made her cry, and she cried every time I did something new. I tried to please her. Why was she unhappy when I tried to be like her?

As soon as I learned to walk, Mommy stood me against my closet doorframe, made a mark, and wrote "five months." She said, "Your father will want to know." He never came to see us, so why would he want to know? After that, she marked my height every week. She shook her head and cried when she looked at the marks. She had to use a stepladder to make a mark for age six.

She bought me new clothes. I wore children's clothes when I began to walk. Now I wear women's plus sizes. People stare at us, especially at me. But I just smile. I think it's because we speak Russian. We walk in Gerald Park some afternoons. Kids want me to play basketball. But Mommy says no. "But I can easily reach the basket," I tell her. She still says no. I want to go out more, but she's afraid.

I taught myself to read English. I read the newspaper. She said I should watch TV to learn proper English. So I watched Sesame

Street, then Nickelodeon. I looked for news about Russia.

Last week something awful happened. I screamed, "Mommy, there is blood in my pants." She cried again, shaking her head that this shouldn't happen to me now. I thought I was going to die. She stopped crying when she realized how scared I was. *What is happening to me?*

CHAPTER 1

A loud sound shattered Val's sleep. "David, what's that?" Val untangled from her husband and checked the clock-radio on the oak table beside her, realizing she'd heard the doorbell. "It's two a.m. Who's that at this hour?" In the dark, she hurried downstairs ahead of David, nearly sleepwalking, and looked through the peephole in the door.

"It's the tall, red-haired woman from the condo next door! I think her name is Mary. Something must have happened. Turn off the alarm, David, so we can let her in." Val heard the repeated beeps as he entered the code on the panel in the hall. When she opened the front door, a woman stood in the doorway wailing. Val stepped back, and the woman ducked her head to pass under the doorframe.

"Mommy is dead. She woke me up, calling my name. She couldn't breathe. Her throat made awful gagging sounds. I tried to wake her, but she wouldn't. Come see. Please. Please." The woman wore jeans with patches of extra denim sewn to the legs to make them long enough. Her plain navy T-shirt was spotted with tears, and her feet were bare.

Val and David slid into their matching black and white Adidas flip-flops at the front door and followed the woman to the open door of her condo. They followed her up the green carpeted stairs to a bedroom, past an old wooden dresser, to a poster bed.

A woman lay on the bed beneath a bedspread tucked neatly under her chin. Her eyes and mouth were open, and the musty scent of death repelled Val. But she forced herself to move the high collar of the woman's pink gown and pressed two fingers to the side of her neck.

"Yes, she's dead." Val stood awkwardly, and Mary hugged her, sobbing over Val's head. Then she pulled away, mumbling, "My name is Mary Solven." Then she sat on the edge of the bed, and said, "Mommy, Mommy," as she stroked her mother's face.

"I'm so sorry, Mary. Is there anyone we can call for you? Maybe your father?" Val asked. She looked around the room for a phone or pictures that might help identify relatives. "David, I don't see a phone. Can you call 911 from our condo?"

As David hurried out, Val noticed numerous white porcelain figurines on the bedside table and a gilt framed photograph of two young women with red hair.

"That's my mother and me taken a few years ago before she got sick," Mary said, as Val picked up the picture. "I don't have a father."

"What's your mother's name?" Val asked, examining the photograph more closely.

"Erika Solven."

"In this picture, she looks too young to be your mother, Mary. In fact, the two of you look about the same age."

Val handed the photograph to Mary and looking past her, noticed the religious icons and triptychs, some primitive and homemade, that cluttered the walls.

"Look, there's something under the picture," Mary said. She slid several worn pages out of the frame and read silently. Then she held the pages out to Val who saw that the language was foreign, probably Russian, although Val couldn't read it.

"Mommy says here that at her death she gives me to Dr. Val Smythe, the scientist next door. That's you. All Mommy's property and money are mine, but Dr. Val Smythe is appointed as trustee in charge until I reach twenty-one."

"Oh no, there must be some mistake," Val said, brushing a dark hand over her squiggly short hair. She suddenly felt self-conscious in her pajamas, and this diminished her resolve. "I don't know you or your mother, and you're a grown woman who doesn't need my help. How old are you?" The peppery shrimp stew David had served for supper welled in her throat.

"I'll be seven in November." Despite her tears, Mary spoke proudly.

"That's impossible! You're a mature young woman."

David reappeared in the doorway. "They're on their way."

Val turned to him for support. "What's going on here, David? Is this some sort of scam? We should go before we get any more involved."

"I'm not sure what you mean. But I do know this woman is in pain, grieving. Someone needs to be with her." David turned to Mary. "You must have a father. Where is he?"

"He doesn't want me," Mary said. "Mommy wanted me to be with you," she pointed at Val, "and that's what I want."

"OK, Mary, let's save all this for later. We need to take care of your mother," Val said, regaining her composure. "Let's go sit in the living room until the ambulance arrives."

A couch and three chairs had been upholstered in dull, beige cloth. Two matching blond tables flanked the couch, and three other matching tables, one beside each chair, made the room look dull and muted. Identical lamps with flowered patterned bases feigned brightness, but the sameness of everything was almost overwhelming. Val decided she couldn't sit. She walked to one wall that held several small bookcases filled with books. Most of them seemed to be in the same foreign language. Val realized also that her scientific curiosity was working. She wanted Mary to translate more of the letter.

XXXX

Mary had refused to stay in her own condo without her mother, and David convinced Val that it was only humane to let her stay in their upstairs guestroom, and that if she was with them, they'd get to the bottom of this a lot faster. David, the ex-priest, Val thought, never got the "good Samaritan" out of his system.

The next morning, Val awakened to the familiar aroma of coffee, French dark roast—her favorite, with the bitter almost burnt taste she adored. This might be the only normal part of the weekend, she thought, as she pulled on her white terry cloth robe. David liked the contrast of her mocha skin against the white cloth. She heard his voice, and Mary's, as she started down the stairs.

"Well, everyone's up but me. That was a short night wasn't it, sweetheart?" Val said, kissing David and ignoring Mary for the moment, hoping she'd quietly disappear.

David wore khakis and T-shirt, which he covered with an apron to guard against the grease that invariably splattered when he fried anything. Val liked his straight blond hair and fair skin, slightly freckled from the sun, the antithesis of her complexion. His tall frame, lean muscles, and Germanic character reminded her a little of her father. She wondered if young girls who imprinted on their fathers later chose husbands that looked liked their fathers.

"Hey, babe," David said, "not much sleep for sure. But you know me. When I see daylight, I'm awake. That must be true of Mary too." He nodded toward Mary, who sat by a window, absorbed in watching something outside.

"Coffee may restore my civility."

David retrieved a white stoneware cup from the cabinet, filled it, and finished making breakfast. David and Val ate at their glass-topped dining table in a nook of the kitchen overlooking the courtyard. There was only room for two people, and Mary was too large to eat at the table anyway, so she ate from a breakfast tray on her lap. Even seated, Mary's unusual size was obvious. Everything about her was large, but proportionally so. She was beautiful, perhaps a Russian basketball player, Val considered. She'd confront Mary as soon as they finished breakfast.

"Mary, what does the rest of the letter say, and what language is it in? Russian?" Val asked.

"Yes. I'll get it from the bedroom upstairs and be right back, Mommy Val." Mary put her tray in the kitchen and went upstairs.

"Don't call me that!" Val yelled as she left the room. "I'm not your mother. Trustee and mother aren't the same!"

"Val, be nice. The girl's mother just died," David said softly.

Mary came back from the bedroom. She'd been crying again. She wiped her eyes with one hand and read them the letter. To Val's dismay, Mary repeated that she was born six years ago. Her father was Dr. Maximilian Solven, and he had left town after Mary was born. He owned the Solven Fertility Clinic in Houston and refused to answer Mrs. Solven's calls about her eminent death from cancer.

"Solven Fertility Clinic? Isn't that the clinic we went to in Houston, David?"

David nodded, not wanting to divert Mary from reading the letter. But Val's thoughts drifted there, to the time when they had consulted a doctor at Solven Fertility Clinic. But that doctor wasn't Solven, a name she hadn't previously associated with a doctor, just the clinic. Their doctor, Samuels, had told them that although David produced good sperm, they weren't able to fertilize her ova. The recommended procedure was *in vitro* fertilization. Sperm would be extracted from his testes and mixed in a Petri dish with eggs from her ovary. The embryos would be implanted into Val's uterus. However, they never got to the procedure. Or, rather, the time was never right for Val. Research was her baby, and she knew that David wouldn't push her. The sixty hours a week she devoted to work didn't allow time for bearing a child, much less caring for one. So they hadn't pursued it.

"Mommy told me I was born in my father's clinic when it was in Vermilion. Wait, I'll get my birth certificate from next door. It has all that information." Mary dashed out the door, ducking under the doorframe.

When she returned, she held not only her birth certificate but a stack of other papers. The signing physician on the birth certificate was Dr. Maximilian Solven, and her remarkable birth date was six years ago in November.

David said, "Well, I'll be a monkey's uncle. Would you look at that?"

Val was appalled. Why would someone put such a completely preposterous date on the birth certificate? Anyone looking at Mary could see the certificate was a forgery, although admittedly, a good one.

"Mary, who forged this birth certificate? It indicates that Mary Solven was six years old last November. You are not six years old."

"But this is the only birth certificate I have. Mommy gave it to me before she died. She said no one would believe it. I guess she was right."

"Yes, she was! We don't believe it," Val said, looking over at David for agreement. "Six-year-olds can't read, and you can read fluent Russian and speak English. How do you explain that?"

Mary pulled out a stack of color photographs held together by a green rubber band. "Here's a picture of me taken when I was a baby." She pointed at the date and handed the photo to Val. "We were on a picnic in the park in St. Martinville. Mommy bought Popeye's fried chicken, and we fed some biscuit crumbs to the ducks."

"Mary, according to that date you would have been five months old. I can't believe that! The child in this picture is already walking. I'm just about fed up with this nonsense. I think you need to go." Val stood up from her chair at the dining table.

"No, please, please. There's more in the letter to translate for you. Listen: 'I chose Dr. Val Smythe to take care of Mary because she's a scientist and can find out what's wrong with my girl. Mary was born a normal baby after only three months in my body, and she grew up too fast.' See, Mommy explains everything in the letter."

"Yes, I get the idea. Your mother was in on this conspiracy too." Val interrupted the reading and began shuffling through the papers Mary had placed on the dining table.

"But I have no family now. Who will take care of me?" Mary began to sob.

David went to Mary's chair and put his arm around her. "We'll figure something out. Don't worry."

"David, she can't live with us. She's obviously lying about her age, and her mother was in on this scheme. For all we know, she might have killed her mother, or the woman she's calling her mother."

Mary suddenly stood, dwarfing Val. "I did not harm Mommy."

The three of them now stood together, silent for a moment.

"OK," Val said. "I didn't mean that. But I can't begin to figure out what she, your mother I mean," looking at Mary, "thought you would get out of this."

"Val, I think we should let Mary stay until we know that answer. There's something about her. Yes, she's big, but she seems young to me, dependent, almost naive. Maybe it's from being sheltered by her mother. Who knows? But I don't think she means us any harm."

Val wasn't sure why, but she also felt herself believing that Mary didn't mean them any harm. She was also becoming intrigued by the seeming contradiction of Mary's womanly beauty and her childlike gestures. She didn't act her age.

"OK, you can stay, Mary, but just until we find out who you really are."

"Thanks, Mommy Val."

"Mary," David said, "do you need anything from your condo? Toothbrush, perhaps? I'll walk over with you and wait outside."

When Mary and David returned, Val was sitting at her desk in the living room. Their condo was too small for a private office, but they hadn't really needed one. David went to his photography studio five days a week and had no interest in working on shop stuff at home. Instead, he read and gardened. So Val used the one desk to prepare her lectures for her university classes. Although she and David had agreed that as soon as she was tenured, they'd sell the condo and buy something bigger, they hadn't made the time to shop around yet.

"Mary, you can put your things in the guestroom upstairs. If you need help, call to us."

"Thank you, Mommy Val."

When Mary was gone, Val said, "What do you think about her, David?"

"Seems she's scamming us, but… What does she hope to gain?"

"I've wracked my brain trying to figure that out, and something about the story rings true. I think I saw Erika with a smaller red-haired girl after they moved into the condo."

"Are you thinking that child was Mary?"

"Maybe… Then what became of that child, David?"

XXYY

"Today, we begin the topic of polyploidy," Val said to her Evolutionary Biology class. This course was required for biology majors, but not for pre-med, nursing, and education students. So the class was usually small—this term a manageable twenty-five students. Her General Biology class, which she taught in the spring was required for all biology majors, and could swell to hundreds. With that many students, you didn't teach, you performed. Dorman Hall had theater seating and dimmed lights, so it was easy to get in the mood. At first, she complained to David that she didn't get to know many of her students in a class that size. But then she realized that eventually, if they took her advanced courses, held in smaller rooms, she'd get to know as many of them as she wanted to know.

"*Poly* means *many* and *ploid* refers to *sets* of chromosomes. So, *polyploids* have more than two sets of chromosomes per cell. You remember from your freshman biology class that living organisms have either one set or two sets of chromosomes in their cells. Human beings have two sets and are referred to as diploid. The prefix *di* means *two*. The two sets carry identical genes, although often different *alleles*, different *forms*, of the same genes.

"To refresh your memories, gametes are the haploid ova and sperm. Cells that have one set of chromosomes, only one copy of each gene, are called haploid. Diploid mother cells in the ovaries and testes divide by meiosis to produce haploid gametes. You should be more than familiar with meiosis from General Bio."

Val suddenly recalled the simplified version of meiosis, explained to them at the Solven Clinic. She had listened patiently for David's sake.

To refocus her own attention and hope to recapture theirs, she posed a question. "Gametes fuse together to form a zygote, or fertilized ovum. So, if each gamete has one set of chromosomes and they fuse to form a zygote, how many sets of chromosomes will the zygote have?"

Several hands went up. She quickly pointed to Nabil, a bright Lebanese student who seemed to get along with everyone. His wealthy parents had sent him to the U.S. to protect him from the turmoil in Lebanon.

"Two," Nabil answered.

"That's right. Diploid zygotes, in our human example, implant in the uterine wall where they grow into embryos, and so on." Except when your husband's sperm avoid your ova for some reason, Val was interrupted by her own thoughts. Then she hurried on.

"However, polyploids have more than two sets of chromosomes and result from a mistake, a grand mutation. Most of the time, this mistake is unsuccessful, so the zygote never develops into an embryo, or if it does, the embryo dies at some point. Zygotes with more than two sets of chromosomes are formed when sperm or ovum or both have more than one set of chromosomes."

She wrote on the board.

2 sets + 1 set = 3 sets in the zygote
(diploid + haploid = triploid)

2 sets + 2 sets = 4 sets in the zygote
(diploid + diploid = tetraploid)

"Cells with three sets of chromosomes are *triploid,* and those with four sets are *tetraploid.* In *Eupatorium,* the group of plants that I've been studying, polyploidy is commonplace. As in this formula, some plants have cells with three, and others plants have cells with four sets of chromosomes, or are triploid and tetraploid, respectively."

She pointed to the board. "I also found that the polyploid races in *Eupatorium* are incapable of reproducing sexually. They produce seeds with cloned embryos inside. New plants growing from these seeds are identical to their parent. In other words, these polyploid plants are parthenogenetic, or apomictic, as it's called in plants."

She noticed some eyes beginning to glaze. "This would be like women having babies spontaneously without sex. Imagine that!"

A male student blurted, "You mean like the virgin birth of Jesus?"

"I don't intend to discuss religion in this class. But I can say that if Jesus were a clone, he would be female," she said. "Let's move on to science, and things we can demonstrate."

Weird human and animal stories always peaked their interest. She continued, "Worms, salamanders, trout, goldfish, mollies, and spiny loach have polyploid races. Polyploidy has never been found in birds or mammals, including human beings. Animals that are polyploid are either sterile, or reproduce by a type of cloning. And it gets stranger.

"For example, polyploids of mole salamanders and black molly fish like the kind sold in pet stores are all female. In order to reproduce they have to steal sperm and use these to trigger egg development. Then they discard the sperm DNA."

She had gotten their attention. Several students stopped taking notes and raised their heads to look at her.

"Polyploidy has its advantages, despite the inability to sexually reproduce. For instance, polyploids are larger, reproduce by cloning at an early age, tolerate colder temperatures, and endure environmental stress." Taller, mature earlier... what had she left out?

A bizarre idea struck her, like a piece of Celotex falling from the ceiling, which was possible in this classroom. Could Mary be polyploid? She's taller than normal and matured early. Was she created in her father's fertility clinic? She had to see her chromosomes and talk to Dr. Solven. Or was she being ridiculous? If she mentioned this to her colleagues, they'd say she'd been running too many miles in the park.

Val became aware of the puzzled looks from the students. How long had she been lost in her own thoughts? She looked at the clock. Twenty minutes of class remained. "This is a good place to stop," she said, disregarding the absurdity of her hypothesis.

She was jumping to conclusions, she thought as she left the classroom. And she was being most unscientific. But her intuition had helped her solve problems before, and she couldn't ignore it. Einstein valued intuition, and Val had memorized his famous quotation: "It is better for people to be like the beasts. They should be more intuitive; they should not be too conscious of what they are doing while they are doing it."

As she rushed from Bodin Hall, she dialed Walt Klein about the "Mary Project." There—she'd already titled the work. How convenient that Walt worked with primate chromosome genetics. His graduate student could do Mary's karyotype if Walt didn't want to. First, however, Val had to convince Walt.

She waited for traffic to stop at the crosswalk on St. James Street and checked her reception bars. Four out of five. Walt answered in his slight German accent. She imagined him picking up his pipe and striking a match. Val rather liked the slight chocolaty scent of his tobacco. But she wondered how much longer he'd get away with smoking over the loud complaints.

"I quit early, which made them happy," Val answered when Walt asked why she wasn't in class. "I have an idea to talk over with you." Val loved the anticipation of impending discovery, but normally guarded her ideas from colleagues so often motivated by jealous impulses. She knew she was too sensitive, but what could she do? Thank God, Walt was entirely too self-assured to be jealous. He told her he'd be in his office all afternoon working on a paper.

At the elevator of Judice Hall, she hesitated. Usually, for exercise, she climbed the five flights of stairs. After the rain, mud had been tracked onto its floor. Val thought about the old Mississippi River dropping its muddy silt load to build southern Louisiana eons ago. She imagined water rushing from the nozzle of a garden hose turned loose in the yard. The hose waved back and forth like a cobra spewing, like the old river swishing back and forth across the landscape of Louisiana spewing mud.

She hardly remembered walking the empty polished hallway from the elevator. Dropping her briefcase with lecture materials inside her office door, Val hurried to Walt's office and found him scrutinizing rows of numbered pictures of chromosomes with colored bands, neatly arranged by size, from longest to shortest. She didn't recognize the karyotype as human, since the end chromosome was numbered 48.

Walt ran his hand through his curly mop of hair that perfectly matched the red of his short beard. He was as usual in wrinkled corduroy pants and white shirt, with brightly colored tie and leather sandals. Only his tie varied from day to day. Today it was yellow with splash patterns of dark green and brown. His small office contained a disheveled desk, crowded bookcases around the wall, his leather chair, and accompanying guest chair, which Val now occupied. The white board on the open wall showed notes in red and yellow where the chromosomes were projected.

As if describing a miracle happening before his eyes, he said, "Man has 46 chromosomes. But his nearest relatives *Pongo* and *Gorilla* have 48. So in the evolution of humans, two chromosomes were lost. Those chromosomes had to have fused with others. I want to know where the genes moved." If she didn't stop him, he would go on about his own work the rest of the afternoon and evening.

She interrupted. "Walt, I think I've found a polyploid human being. She's a six-year-old living next door to me. Mary is almost seven feet tall and still growing. She's a perfectly healthy looking human being, not distorted in appearance like a person with a growth disorder. I want you to culture her blood cells for karyotype analysis. I'd do it myself, but I don't have the experience with animal karyotypes that you do."

He was wide-eyed but sat silently. He leaned back in his chair, emphasizing his growing middle, and made a half-effort to relight his pipe. She felt like someone who had admitted to her psychiatrist that she was probably insane and awaited the verdict.

"Walt, please speak up! I know how much this flies in the face of your beliefs. But what else could it be?"

"Val, I know polyploidy is a way of life with you. But humans aren't plants, and even if a polyploid were conceived, it would have aborted. The imbalance of chromosomes and genes would doom normal development. Besides, with multiple sex chromosomes, there's the problem of sexual expression. This woman, I mean girl, must have an undiagnosed metabolic disorder."

"But she's not sick, Walt." Val knew from experience that Walt had to unload his own opinions before considering hers. Eventually, he'd be swayed by his respect for her, even though animal chromosomes were his territory and not hers.

"Humor me, Walt. It won't take you that much time. Even if she's not polyploid, she might have some other chromosomal anomaly that would interest you."

"OK, I'll let you know. I'm busy right now. Maybe my graduate student, Ken, can do the work. Don't worry. I'll look over his shoulder." Walt fiddled with his pipe, finally relighting it.

CHAPTER 2

"Hello, this is Dr. Val Smythe. May I speak with Dr. Maximilian Solven, please?" Val closed her office door so she wouldn't be overheard.

The receptionist told Val that the doctor couldn't take her call and asked if she could help. "I'm calling from Vermilion, Louisiana about his daughter, Mary Solven. She's currently living with me. Her mother has died, and I need to know what to do with her."

There was a long silence. Then the receptionist said, "One moment, please." When she came back on the line she said, "Dr. Solven will call you back."

Val gave her cell number. "There's something I'd like to ask you. Mary's a full-grown woman, but she insists she's only six years old. Is that possible?"

The woman told Val that it was and hung up abruptly.

Val was stunned. Mary *could* be polyploid. How else to explain a nearly seven-foot tall six-year-old? How would the receptionist know anything about Mary? Her polyploidy must have something to do with her father's fertility clinic.

A few minutes later Val's cell phone rang a few notes of Beethoven.

"Yes, this is Dr. Val Smythe." She struggled to understand his heavy accent. "I need to talk to you about your daughter, Mary." ... "No, I don't have time to fly to Houston to meet with you. Can't you answer my questions over the phone?" ... "Is she really six years old as she claims?" ... "What? Then how did she grow up so fast?" ... "Fine, she's special. But why?" ... "Answer my question. I'm sure you know."

Dr. Solven cut her off. She would have to come to Houston if she wanted any more answers. But why waste her time?

A week later, Val and Mary, shaded by massive live oaks in the courtyard surrounding the condos, sat on concrete benches, arguing. "I know how I look. But I want to go to school like other children." Mary began crying. "They could get me a bigger desk. I could help the teacher carry things that other kids couldn't. I could help other kids move their desks or get things they couldn't reach."

Val's attitude toward Mary had changed abruptly since she'd decided Mary might be polyploid and, she reluctantly admitted to herself, *of scientific interest.* She had taken the day off to spend time with her. She guessed this was how it was for mothers, although not exactly, considering the strangeness of this "child." But Mary's dependence on Val was child-like, in contradiction to her adult appearance.

"Mary, the school principal won't believe you're six years old," Val explained.

"Mommy said I could go to school when I was six. So why can't I?" Mary began to cry again. Val knew she cried for her mother as well as from disappointment. Val hugged her until she stopped crying. She took Mary's hand and resumed the conversation using another tactic.

"Do you remember yesterday when we saw Tommy outside the condo, and you wanted to talk to him? He called you 'Miss Mary,' because he thought you were a grown-up." Val looked at Mary.

"Yes, I know what he thought. But I'm not. I'm the same age as him. I know because he starts school in September," Mary said.

How could she ever explain Mary's situation to her? She couldn't understand it herself.

"Mary, stand up beside me. See, I have to look up to see your face. You're much taller than I am. You know this, but try to imagine what other people think."

"I'll tell them I want to learn to read and do arithmetic."

"But, Mary, you *can* read and do arithmetic! You read books and newspapers. Children your age can't do that! Besides, you'd be bored in school.

"Why can't other children read?"

"Children can't do the arithmetic that you can in the first grade. Except if they're geniuses," Val said, realizing she'd given Mary an opportunity for further debate.

"Where do geniuses go to school, then? That's where I want to go," Mary said. The intense blue of her eyes deepened.

"They skip grades until they reach their level of skill."

"That's what I want to do. What is my level, Mommy Val?"

"Your situation is different from other child geniuses. When they're still very young their minds are like yours, at an adult level, but their bodies are immature," Val explained.

"I get it. My body is way ahead like their minds. But my mind is way ahead too." Mary did seem to get it.

"Yes, your mind and body are geniuses," Val said softly.

XXYY

Val's parents, Hank and Belle, expected them for Sunday dinner in Arath. So they decided to bring Mary. Belle always cooked more food than the four of them could eat and would welcome Mary with open arms. Hank would be happy to tell his stories to someone new. Val planned to say that Mary's mother had died recently, and Mary needed a change of scene. She'd tell them more when she needed to.

David drove them south, through the vast flat prairie land of South Louisiana now under cultivation. It was spring, and the fields of rice surrounding the small town of Arath were green. Later in the year, after the golden tips of the crops were harvested, the fields would be flooded for crawfish. The dome-shaped crawfish traps, looking like miniature space capsules, were anchored in rows throughout the fields with only the red tops above water. Throughout the winter months, the bright tops were a welcome contrast to the brown landscape. Val's dad baited his traps with frozen fish, although others used chicken, cat food, and just about any other meat. The important thing was to use oily meat that produced a heavy scent to attract the crawfish.

Val's thoughts turned to Mary, who stretched out in the back seat, quietly absorbed in her book. "I was lonely growing up here, David. I was different, like Mary in a way. Arath seemed tolerant of my brown skin, but my classmates were white. I was never invited to their houses for birthday parties or sleepovers."

David pulled her toward him as far as the seat belts of their Honda Accord would allow. "I know it was hard for you growing up here. That's why you empathize with Mary. All we can do is love and care for her, like your parents did for you. It's like having a child of our own without the diaper phase," David said, and they both laughed.

"You always know how to cheer me up. I guess I'm too serious, but my life has been so different than yours. That's why you're good for me, white boy."

The red brick, two-story high school building loomed along the short main street of Arath. Blue and gold banners hung over the school marquee. Early on, teachers had encouraged Val to explore and excel. As soon as she was old enough to shoot baskets, the basketball coach had recruited her. She was exceptionally tall—six feet two inches by her senior year. That was the year she set a district scoring record. She guessed her life as a minority had turned out better than for many. But Mary might even be more different. And the more unlike everyone else Mary was, the less optimistic Val felt about the future.

Hank and Belle were waiting on the porch. They always seemed happy, but Val knew how difficult their marriage had been, living in a small town. Belle's parents had forbidden her to marry Hank, but he had persisted. They met on Mardi Gras morning at the Café Mundo in New Orleans when he and some friends from Arath arrived hungry for beignets and chicory coffee. He loved telling the story, and Val could almost recite it by heart. "Yes Dad, a true romance. You should write it down and send it to a magazine."

"Now, Val," Hank said, "Mary wants to hear it." He smiled at the tall girl sitting across from him during dinner. "Belle was at the table next to mine, her skin shimmering in the morning light. White powdered sugar from the beignets sprinkled her dark hands and nose a little. And she smiled the most beautiful smile I ever saw. That's how it all started," he said, cherishing the memory. "I married her a few weeks later and brought her home to the family farm."

Val had wonderful memories of visiting her Benoit grandparents in New Orleans during Christmas holidays and summers, but they had died when she was in high school. They lived on Dauphine Street in the Fauberg Marigny section of New Orleans in one of the many ornate century-old cottages that lined the street. The smells of fine cooking wafted through the neighborhood. Even today, the odors of certain New Orleanian specialties like shrimp Creole and andouille-okra gumbo brought memories of her grandparents.

Val's mother insisted that Hank drive her to New Orleans to see her old home just weeks after Hurricane Katrina. Belle still had a soft spot for the old place, even though she and her sister had sold it after their mother died because neither of them wanted to live in New Orleans. The house had been spared flood damage. The higher elevation of the old French Quarter, including Fauberg Marigny, as well as the raised architecture of the nineteenth-century homes, had saved them from the flood.

Val's Smythe grandparents died before she was born, and she knew them only from stories and a few photographs. At her grandparents wedding, her great grandfather Smythe handed his son a bag of gold he had hidden during the war, along with a paper with written instructions on how to escape Germany through France and travel to New Orleans. This was the summer of 1919, just as the Treaty of Versailles was being signed. Because their home in Germany bordered Alsace-Lorraine, France, they spoke fluent French, and the French speaking area of Louisiana seemed like a natural destination.

From New Orleans, they moved to the rich Louisiana prairie lands to farm. Hank looked almost exactly like his tall, lean, and blond father in the photos. Val's short, plump, great grandmother wore her light colored hair in a bun and tied an apron around her waist. She stood unsmiling beside her husband. German was the language spoken in their home, and Hank had been able to help Val with high school German.

Mary did enjoy Hank's stories, and she encouraged him to continue each time he paused to take a bite of buttery crawfish étouffée. Then later, dishes done, they all talked about crops and farming. If Hank and Belle wanted to know more about Mary, they didn't ask. When the afternoon was half gone, Belle gave Val a couple of pounds of frozen peeled crawfish tails, and they were on their way, a family returning home to the city.

Later, in Delcambre, they stopped at a seafood outlet along the waterfront. The smell of raw seafood was overpowering. Shrimp boats anchored across the road carried tons of ice and spent days offshore before returning with their catch. This was a good year, but years averaged out. Shrimping wasn't a moneymaker. Hurricanes and storms damaged the boats and nets, and it was hard to make a living. Val wanted to support the industry, so she and David liked to buy here, close to the source, when they could. Shrimp, crabs, and flounder.

XXXX

The following morning, Val felt she especially needed to run after all she'd eaten the day before. As she was leaving, Mary appeared in shorts that made her legs look even longer and more beautiful. "May I run with you, Mommy Val?"

Val didn't know what to say. She preferred to run alone. But Mary was dressed, ready to go, and seemed intent. So Val's swelling arguments subsided. After all, running would distract Mary from lingering grief.

As Val preferred, they ran without talking, and as usual, Val started slowly before reaching what she considered a fine pace of eight-minute miles. There was almost no traffic, and they crossed street after street before reaching the park's exercise path where a number of other people were jogging. As Val and Mary passed them, most turned to take in Mary's red hair, size, and beauty. Mary also looked joyful, and she delighted in leaping into the air to touch the branches of live oaks that were higher than most people could reach. After a few loops around the park, small crowds began to gather to watch "the giant," and it wasn't long before Val began to worry about the attention they were attracting.

The next time they ran together, Mary took the lead and led Val across streets and into the park, but not to the running trail. As Val followed behind more slowly, she realized Mary had stopped at a basketball court. Val watched from a distance. Mary greeted several teenage boys who acted as if they knew her. In a moment, she was in a pickup game.

One of the taller boys shouted instructions to Mary, who caught on immediately. She couldn't dribble well, but after a few awkward attempts, she dunked the basketball. Several younger boys who were watching from the edge of the court whooped. Mary beamed, clearly pleased to be part of the group.

The noisy enthusiasm attracted others from a nearby court, and several older boys came over to check out the newcomer. The leader, deliberately cool, dribbled a basketball while he looked at Mary. Then he called out, "You, giant girl, where you from?"

Before Mary could respond, Val stepped forward and yelled, "Mary, we have to go now. David is waiting."

"You gonna let her, a black mama, tell you what to do?" the boy said. "Where's your other mama, the white one, dat talked funny? She ain't liking us either."

The boy turned back to his friends to emphasize his cool. Much to Val's relief, Mary was already walking toward Val. Then she stopped, turned, and said, "See you later, Jacque."

XXYY

The court had recognized Erika Solven's will, and although Val had listed Mary's condo for sale, Mary visited there every day. Val often found Mary crying beside her mother's bed. Mary seemed to be two people, an almost grown woman and a child who needed assurance that she wouldn't be abandoned.

Fortunately, David ran his own photography shop, and he could have Mary there, where she attracted little attention. She quickly learned how to operate duplicating, enlarging, and printing machines. And to David's surprise, she seemed to know intuitively how to correct and improve the color of a photograph and to crop for better composition. It seemed she knew how or could learn to do anything she wanted to. She also liked to go grocery shopping with Val. So they went late, usually just before the store closed when there were few other shoppers.

That evening, as they walked the aisles of the Big Star Grocery, Val listened as Mary kept a running calculation. "That's $2.99 for the tomatoes, $1.29 for onions, equals $4.28, plus $3.69 for broccoli, equals $7.97, plus $4.49 for asparagus equals $12.46."

Val interrupted her. "What are you doing, Mary?"

"I'm keeping track of our total. Mommy taught me the numbers, and when she realized I could add so quickly, she asked me to always add up the cart to make sure we didn't spend too much." She paused, her pleased expression disappearing. "You don't want me to help, Mommy Val?"

"Oh no, I want you to help. I'm just amazed at what you can do."

Val noticed that a woman had moved close and seemed to be listening to them. The woman continued to lurk nearby as they shopped, and finally stepped closer. "I'm Chris," she said, holding out her hand to Val. "I noticed you all when you came into the store, and I've been eavesdropping. Sorry, I don't mean to frighten you. But I've seen others like your daughter here."

"I'm Val, and this is Mary."

Chris said, "I'd like to talk to you about children who grow up too fast, like Mary. Do you have time to meet me next door for coffee? I think you'll be interested in what I have to say."

Val didn't like intrusions in public places, but she was curious, and anything that might help explain Mary was worth exploring. She surprised herself; she said yes.

XXXX

Chris waved to Val and Mary as they walked into Starbucks. They sat down at the table that she had saved for them. Chris smiled continuously through her heavy makeup. "Happy fat lady" came to mind before Val could censor the thought. But the cliché fit. She wore a quarter sleeved denim dress with large brown buttons down the front, which would be loose fitting on anyone else.

Starbucks was packed with high school band students grabbing lattes before going home after practice. They fascinated Mary, and Val realized she must be lonely for the company of young people. Mary's special interest was a tall, swarthy boy standing near their table, and she asked him what he was drinking. He replied in an unnecessarily rude manner that it was a tall latte with whipped cream. Mary didn't seem to notice his rudeness.

"May I taste it?"

"Sure," he said, handing her the cup.

Before she could take it, Val interrupted. "I don't think so, let's get our own. I know you'll like it. Maybe you should get a decaf since you're not used to drinking coffee."

Weaving through the students, Val went to the counter to order. Decaf had to be made, so she went back to the table to wait. They sat quietly for a moment before Mary broke the silence. "Do you have a child like me?" she asked.

"How did you know? Yes, I do, Mary. His name is Jon, and he's seven years old. "

"I just guessed. Is he a genius too, like me? Mommy Val said I'm a genius in mind and body."

"Yes, I guess I'd say he's a genius in ways like you. That's a good way to put it," Chris said.

Other polyploids besides Mary? Wait until Walt hears this.

"Does he go to genius school or to regular school?" Mary asked.

"Neither. His education is from reading books. He's read our books at home and at the city library. Now we go to the university library. Is that what you do?" Chris asked, putting her hand on Mary's arm.

"Yes, me too. Now, I'm reading Mommy Val's science books at her university office. They're mostly about biology, and I like that. Soon I'll be finished with those and go on to the university library. After that, I don't know."

Val noticed their two steaming lattes on the counter. When she returned with the cups, Chris asked, "Do you work at the university?"

"Yes, I'm a biology professor," Val said. "Mary comes to work with me two days a week. Other days she goes with my husband to his photography shop in the Oil Center."

"I'm impressed." Chris paused. "I'm just a housewife. My husband is in the oil business and makes enough so I don't have to work."

"I'm sorry to be pushy," Val looked at her watch, "but it is pretty late. Do you talk to everyone with tall children?"

"Sorry. I just wanted to talk to you. When I heard you talking to Mary like she was a child, I knew she was like my Jon. He's only seven, and I talk to him that way. I thought this might be my chance, so I asked you to come here."

Chris had tears in her eyes. Val looked over at Mary to see how she was responding to the conversation. But she seemed absorbed in the band students who were joking with each other.

Val said, "It's only been a few weeks since Mary's mother died. She lives with my husband and me now. I never knew Mary as a baby, so it's different." Val hoped Mary wasn't upset by mention of her mother, but she was distracted by the boy who had offered her a taste of his latte.

Mary is too young for boys, Val thought, suddenly remembering her own first infatuations. But with Mary's attention elsewhere, she could question Chris more freely. "Was your pregnancy difficult with such a large child?"

"Having Jon would have been impossible without the Solven Fertility Clinic and Dr. Maximilian Solven. We tried for several years to get pregnant before finally deciding to go to the clinic. I think it's moved to Houston. Too bad for women like me in Vermilion."

Val felt goose bumps rise on her arms. Mary's no good father! Should she tell Chris? No, she didn't want to open that can of worms now. Besides, what difference would it make? She needed to think, and they needed to go.

"Thanks for talking to me, Chris. Let's keep in touch. I think you should talk to the other mothers you've seen. They need to know they're not alone."

CHAPTER 2
XXYY

The spicy smell of aftershave alerted Val that her department head was coming down her corridor. Scowling, he barged into her office. "Val, please excuse my directness." He paused for emphasis. "I didn't like the way you answered me about the Leica."

He referred to the microscope in her laboratory. So that's what this is about. What a relief.

She said, "I said in a return note that I didn't want to swap it for a Wild. Next thing, I get a copy of a two-page letter to the dean suggesting I'm insubordinate, and you copied it to the president."

Val turned to Mary who was reading a book. "Mary, please take your books into my lab next door. I'll be there soon."

Jerry's head swiveled to ogle Mary as she went out. "Wow! Who is that gorgeous giant?" he said as he closed the door behind Mary. Then, recovering himself, as if selecting from a repertoire of personalities, he raised his voice in a thick South Georgia accent. "Who in hell do you think you are? You can't tell me how to run this department. I told Barry he could have that microscope, and that's that! I don't need to ask your permission to move equipment."

The top of Jerry's head reached the molding strip over the door. He was well-muscled, balding, and blond. His steel blue eyes glared. His face reddened, and his carotids bulged. Val felt the threat of physical violence fill the shriveled space of her office.

His question about the microscope seemed simple. In the note, he hadn't mentioned that Barry wanted her microscope. Now she understood he needed to save face for his friend, Barry.

"Jerry, wait a minute. I think I misunderstood," she lied. "You weren't really asking if I wanted to trade microscopes." She felt a little sorry for him. Subtle cues from the white male hierarchy are supposed to be recognized and illicit responses that reassure it remains in power. Since she wasn't male or white, any response she gave was viewed as a threat. At least she'd stopped thinking that the "misunderstandings" were her failure. In lighter moments, she had remarked to David that secret information was genetically coded on the Y chromosome.

"Jerry, give the microscope to Barry. OK? I'll use the Wild," Val pronounced it "Vild" the German way.

"Well, alright. I guess in that case, I apologize." Jerry turned to the door. "I hope this doesn't affect our friendship."

After Jerry was out of sight, Val went to see Walt.

"You look upset," Walt said as she entered his office. "I heard Jerry's voice. What happened?"

"Never mind about Jerry. I met a woman in the Big Star who conceived a son like Mary."

"Another one?" Walt's mind jumped to possibility. "Bring Mary, and I'll take some blood. If it will make you happy."

CHAPTER 3

Val and Mary walked to Campeau's Grocery for the Tuesday shrimp Po'Boy special. They sat at one of the tables covered with a checkered cloth. Quietly, they ate French bread rolls slathered with mayonnaise and stuffed with Tabasco spiced fried shrimp.

"What's the matter, Mommy Val? Are you mad at me?"

"Oh no, honey. I'm not mad at you. I'm sorry. I was just thinking." Val looked around to see if anyone had overheard Mary call her Mommy.

"Let's go back to campus. I need to talk to you about something."

They emptied their trays and started back.

"Mary, you know we've discussed before how unusual you are. I think it's because you have multiple sets of chromosomes." She took a deep breath. "You're polyploid. Do you know what chromosomes are, Mary?"

"Yes, I read about it. Human cells have 23 pairs. Chromosomes contain DNA, which carries genes."

"OK, then. I talked to Walt about this already, and he's willing to take a sample of your blood to examine your chromosomes. You can consent to this or not. But I have to tell you that Walt doesn't believe you're polyploid, and he's probably just humoring me."

Mary said uneasily, "I'll do it, but I'm not sure I want to know, Mommy Val. Can we talk about it later?"

Walt was in his lab. "I'm not an expert at taking blood from humans, but you'll be easier than a hairy monkey." He laughed, doing his best to help Mary relax. She sat on the lab stool, and Walt relaxed her forearm down onto the counter. After sterilizing a spot with alcohol, he inserted the syringe, and withdrew a small amount of blood. Mary squirmed, squeezing her eyes shut.

"Done!" Walt said. "Call me a vampire." And when no one laughed, he said, "We'll have results in a week."

He popped off the sample tube from the syringe and pressed a cotton ball against her arm over the puncture. "It takes two to three days to grow the dividing white blood cells, then another day or two for staining and photographing before we have the pictures of your chromosomes."

"I know there can be no polyploid primates. You know I'm not polyploid, Dr. Walt?"

Walt raised his eyebrows. "You're right, Mary, there aren't any primates that are known to be polyploid. But anything is possible, right?"

XXXX

After supper, David went back to his shop to finish a photography project. Before Mary, Val worked every night during the week until at least nine o'clock. No one, including David, had ever distracted her from work the way Mary had. Tonight she should have been working on a grant proposal that was due the following week, but she had to talk with Mary.

They walked past the hedge of camellias. Hundreds of red-petaled flowers of this sterile hybrid cultivar spread wide to reveal empty yellow stamens. Habitually, she classified plants as she passed them—*Camellia*, an Asian genus in the family Theaceae, which also contains the tea species, *Camellia sinensis. Sinensis* meant Chinese for the tea from China. She was often unfamiliar with species names for cultivars and hybrids like this camellia in the courtyard. Often named after the horticulturist who created the hybrids, the names carried less meaning to her.

"I want to talk to you about sex," she began awkwardly.

"What do you want to tell me? I've read all about sex in books, and I've seen pictures. I know that intercourse can lead to pregnancy, HIV, and other infectious diseases." Mary volunteered this information flatly, as if quoting from a textbook.

Val had planned a mini-lecture that included anatomy, puberty, and protection, but now she was suddenly at a loss. "Is there anything else you want to know?" Val asked.

"Yes, what does it feel like?"

That question was not among the mini-lecture topics Val had intended to give, but if that's what she wanted to know, then she'd rather *tell* Mary how sex felt than have her experiment. "In lovemaking," she said slowly, "an overwhelming pleasurable experience called orgasm happens. However, there's a downside or tricky part. A hormone called oxytocin is produced during sex. It's produced at other times too, but for now, let's stick to sex. Oxytocin makes you want to bond to the person you make love with."

"What do you mean by bonding?" Mary asked.

"It means you don't want to be separated from your lover," Val said. "That's why you want to be very careful about choosing a partner. In the old days, sex was forbidden before marriage. Not a bad idea in some ways. But it does suggest you're more rational before having sex."

Val felt like a phony advocating abstinence before marriage. She'd had a brief affair before she met David, and she and David hadn't waited until after marriage. So why did her own behavior seem irrelevant when she explained this to Mary?

"You might be sexually attracted to someone like Jacque. If so, that's OK," Val quickly added, wanting to influence her actions and not make her feel guilty about her feelings. But Jacque was the reason for this conversation. "Sex is different for boys. You know, more casual, but not always. I guess if sex were unpleasant, species, including humans, wouldn't be around long. People can think, which helps us stay out of bad situations."

"I'm not having sex with Jacque and probably won't. He's cute, and I like talking to him, but that's all. Sex is too complicated for me right now. I'm not attracted to anybody. Besides, I could get pregnant, and I'm too young to be a mother."

Val was surprised by Mary's frankness, but relieved. Yet her rational mind knew that sex between Mary and a diploid probably wouldn't result in pregnancy. Why didn't these conversations involving emotions behave more logically?

"That's interesting about oxytocin and bonding," Mary said. "You're saying I might bond with a guy after having sex with him, but not have anything to talk to him about. I can see how that could be a problem."

"Yes, that's what I was getting at."

"I guess bonding ensures that children have two parents," Mary said. "The glue must not have been very sticky between my parents."

Val laughed. "You put that well. Sticky glue is a good metaphor. I guess glue isn't enough. Glue is just glue or oxytocin in this case. Compatibility is something you discover by sharing your hopes, dreams, and anything else really. You fall in love."

"Is that what happened with you and David? You care so much about each other."

"Yes, I fell in love with David, and I fall in love with David over and over. It's strange. I can't explain it, but I can't imagine life without him. Feelings just are, and I'm not sure anyone can explain or control them. Some attractions lead to deeper feelings. Some don't. And some strong attractions turn into something else, sometimes to friendships."

"I understand, Mommy Val. Don't worry. I don't have any strong attractions now, but when I do, I'll remember what you said."

"Because I," Val's voice trailed. "I want you to be happy and never disappointed." She was near tears and surprised at how her feelings about Mary were changing. Volatile. Could she love her? Really? A polyploid?

Mary hugged her tightly. "I love you too, Mommy Val."

XXYY

After work on Friday, Val and David arrived home about the same time.

"Where's Mary?"

"She left the shop about three. Said she left her book at home," David said.

He called Mary's name as they entered the condo.

"Maybe she's at the park," Val said. "Look for a note while I check next door. The Solven condo key is on the hook, so she isn't there." Val noticed that her car key was missing. "I think she's taken my car. I can't believe it, David."

"Where would she go?"

"She asked me to teach her to drive. Of course, I refused, but the last time we were in the car she quizzed me about everything I did."

David checked the phone. Jacque had called.

"She likes Starbucks. Let's try there," Val said.

David grabbed his keys. They looked for Val's car at the park then drove to Starbucks. To their relief, the car was there, parked precisely between the lines.

Through the windows, Val saw Mary and Jacque sipping lattes, heads bent close together. Mary stood when Val and David came in, and Val could see her blushing cheeks from the door. Val wanted to be angry, but she was so relieved she only wanted to hug Mary. The intensity of her feelings surprised her. Were they maternal? If so, where had they been before she met Mary? She'd been concerned about David many times, but now a fear of Mary being harmed was overwhelming, like nothing she'd felt before.

"Mary, why did you take my car without permission? You don't have a license, and I would have driven you to see your friend."

"You and David were busy. Why does it matter? You didn't need your car. I went home to read, but Jacque called and wanted me to meet him here to talk."

Val noticed Mary had dropped the "Mommy."

"Yeah. She's *big* enough to drive," Jacque said, laughing at his joke. "You act like prison guards. You take her to work wit' you. She don't go to school. Dat's crazy." Val recognized the source of Mary's rebellious tone.

"Never mind. This is between Mary and her family," Val said. "Do you have a ride home, Jacque? Did Mary pick you up?"

"No, I rode my bike. I'm going. Be cool. Bye, Mary." Jacque walked out, leaving his steaming latte.

What was Mary's attraction to Jacque? Val wondered. His grammar was awful.

"Mary, we were worried sick not knowing where you were."

"What would you like, Val?" David interrupted. "I'm having

tuna salad on a croissant."

Val took a deep breath. "Me too, thanks. Mary?"

"Chicken salad on a croissant, please," Mary said, warming to the idea of food.

David went to the counter to place the order.

"About the driving, Mary," Val said. "Besides not having a driver's license, there are other complications. Your birth certificate, for one. Obviously you can drive, but not legally."

"Why not? That doesn't make sense."

"But it's the law."

David returned to the table. "Val, considering Mary's situation, maybe we should get her a new birth certificate."

"You mean forge one?" Val whispered. "That's illegal!"

"In the photography business you get all kinds of requests."

"Do you mean you do forgeries?"

"So it's OK to have a forged birth certificate, but not to drive a car without a license?" Mary asked.

Spoken like a typical teenager, Val thought. Mary could be so sweetie pie with: "I love you, Mommy Val." Now it was: "Explain your logic, or I won't love you."

"That seems to be David's opinion," Val said. "Let's talk about your work later, David. You're scaring me."

"Why do I have to live with you and David anyway? I have my own condo. I think I'll live there by myself," Mary said.

"Mary, you don't mean that. You're angry. Besides, I won't let you," Val said.

"How will you stop me? Call Child Protection. What'll they say when they see me? You can't do anything but make a lot of trouble if you try to keep me from moving out."

"That's a great idea, Mary," David said. "You're a grown woman. So why don't you live in your own place? The birth certificate you have is probably a fake anyway. You can't be six. Look at you."

Val was shocked. "You've been sitting on this, haven't you, David?" Val said louder than she had intended. People turned from their tables to stare. Everyone wanted to eat in peace.

"Calm down, Val. Look at the evidence. You're the scientist. Be objective." David had a point. But all the evidence wasn't in yet.

"OK, David. I see what you mean, as far as it goes. But there's more evidence to come: the chromosome count Walt is working on." Was David serious or playing devil's advocate?

"Whether Mary is polyploid or not, our rules and laws don't apply to her. Don't you see?"

"David understands better than you do, *Mommy* Val. I wasn't very nice about it, but I have to find my own way. And it's not going to be like a normal person."

Val looked at her with new eyes. This is how it feels when parents have to let their child go, she thought. "I think we should go home, now. Or rather to our homes, if that's the way you want it, Mary."

On the way out, Val's phone rang. "Hello?" ... "Is that you, Walt? I can't understand you. Speak English." ... "What!"

She turned to Mary. "You are officially the most unusual person I know, Mary. You're polyploid, tetraploid to be exact, with four sets of chromosomes." But the look on Mary's face made her realize she'd been insensitive. "Mary, this is good news. Look what you can do that we can't. You're stronger, smarter, and grow up faster. You're a super human."

"I know, Mommy Val... Mommy was right that you would figure out what was wrong with me. But I just want to be normal and live a normal life."

"Maybe there are more polyploids like you. Remember what Chris said about her son? And Walt can help us get to the bottom of this."

XXXX

On a wall outside Walt's office, pictures of thick, linear structures with colored bands were aligned from longest to shortest. Inside, a similar chart was projected on the whiteboard across the room. Walt stood beside the board, filling it with equations.

"Look, 96 chromosomes," Walt said. "I've never seen anything like it. But I'll have to take another sample to be absolutely sure."

"How did they double the chromosomes?" Val asked.

33

"I don't know. The chromosomes could have been replicated in ova and sperm or in the fertilized egg." Then looking at David and Mary, he said, "Let me try to explain."

Walt held a red marker in one hand and a laser pointer in the other. "Mary is 4X, tetraploid. She has four sets of each of her chromosomes. These are her four sex chromosomes." Walt pointed to a group of four X-shaped chromosomes in the display. He wrote XXXX on the board under Mary's chromosomes.

"But I need to see a polyploid carrying one or more Y chromosomes in order to determine how they created polyploids. Such an individual may have two X chromosomes and two Y chromosomes. Or the individual could be XXXY or XYYY." He wrote XXYY and the two other possibilities on the board. "If a Y-carrying individual has an odd number of Y's, then they tripled the chromosomes in the ova or the sperm. If there's an even number, then they doubled the chromosomes in the fertilized egg, or less likely, they doubled the chromosomes in both the ova and the sperm."

"Aren't all Y-carrying individuals male?" David asked.

"Good question, David. Yes and no. I say this because diploid humans with one extra sex chromosome XXY exist who are intersexual. That is, they have both male and female secondary characteristics.

"That makes sense, Walt," Val said. "I told you about talking to Chris in Big Star. Chris said her son was like Mary. Also, her pregnancy was *in vitro* at the Solven Clinic. She didn't seem ambiguous about her son's sex. Her concerns were his rapid growth, size, and advanced intellect."

"If there are no real polyploid males, I won't be able to have a family, will I?" Mary said.

"I must see his chromosomes. Can you get him here?" Walt asked.

"I'm sure we can," Val said. "But do you have any idea how they did it? I've used colchicine and other agents to stop division of cells, which, if the cells lived, would have been polyploid, but the process kills cells."

"Yes. The methods commonly used for doubling chromosome numbers are lethal to cells," Walt said.

"Do the chromosomes look normal? Have they been altered?" Val asked.

They both knew this was the discovery of a lifetime, and Walt's appearance showed it. Uncombed red hair sprang in all directions, and his blue eyes gleamed.

"They appear to be normal, except for number, but we won't know for sure until I've done a few more analyses."

"You're going to be famous, Mary," David said. "I was wrong about your birth certificate being a forgery. You're a child's age, but an adult. I think we can all see that. I'll work on a new birth certificate.

"I just want a normal life, go to school, and have a family someday. I don't want to be a circus freak, like in *The Elephant Boy*. I'm not disfigured, and Chris' son is like me. And if there are others." She paused. "Then I'm not a freak at all!"

XXYY

The next morning, Val woke to the familiar smell of dark roast coffee and heard David and Mary talking in the kitchen. Mary had said she was too frightened to be alone and had stayed in their condo after all.

Val joined them in the kitchen. "Good morning, David, my lovely man." Val wrapped her arms around him and gave him a sleepy morning breath kiss, which he didn't seem to mind. "Mary, how did you sleep?"

Mary smiled. All was forgiven. Family, that's what it was like, Val thought, remembering her Creole family.

"Mommy Val, I want to visit Chris and her son. Can we go today?"

"Today isn't good for me. I have classes and a grant proposal to finish before Friday. How about tomorrow?"

"I could visit them on my own. Chris could come here, or I could walk to her house. I promise not to drive until I get a license. David is making me a birth certificate so I can take the test."

"So that's what you two have been conspiring about this

morning. Don't you need a social security number first? Never mind. Don't answer that. David is the expert on forgeries," Val said. "I'll leave you two to conspire while I get dressed."

CHAPTER 4

Mary called Chris as soon as Val and David left for work. "Hello, this is Mary Solven. We met at Big Star, and you said you had a son like me. Do you remember?" … "Good, I was wondering if I could meet your son." Mary had taken a bold step, and she knew how Val would react to it.

"I can walk to your house. I walk fast. Or you could come here. I live near the university on Gerald Drive, next to the park." Chris said they'd see her soon.

Soon! Mary's heart was racing. She hadn't expected this to work so smoothly. She needed to get ready for them. What would he look like? Would he be taller than she was? Should she serve juice? Coffee or tea? She found half a blueberry pie in the refrigerator from last night's supper, but that wouldn't be good with orange juice, would it? She'd ask what they preferred. That's how David would do it. She'd follow his example.

Mary showered, dressed in her newest pair of jeans, a sleeveless blue blouse to complement her red hair, and sandals. She waited in the living room reading *The Secrets of Pi*. She'd also started a book on number theory. She wanted to know everything. Maybe she'd be able to talk to mathematicians at the university? Maybe Chris' son read math books? Her mind was racing.

The doorbell rang. She took a deep breath and tried not to rush to the door. There stood the most handsome man she'd ever seen. He was swarthy, somehow natural looking, she thought, with the blackest hair and eyes she'd ever seen.

Somehow she managed to speak. "I'm Mary Solven," she said and held out her hand.

"This is Jon, my son." Chris stepped up to his side.

Mary felt dizzy. She leaned against the doorframe to regain her balance, hoping they hadn't noticed. What was happening to her? Was this the chemistry Val had told her about? "Sorry," Mary said. "Please come in."

Jon ducked his head into the doorway and entered as if into a dollhouse. Mary motioned them toward the couch, and she sat in a nearby rocking chair. Chris looked nervously around the room, while Jon sat staring at Mary. Mary seemed to have forgotten her good hostess plan.

Chris broke the silence. "I'm confused. I thought Val would be here. I have some news for her, about other parents of children like you and Jon. Did you say your last name was Solven? Are you related to Dr. Solven?"

"Yes. He's my father."

"Just as I suspected," Chris said. "Your family is responsible for this."

"I'm not sure what you mean by responsible. But I know my father is a genius. And I know, thanks to Dr. Walt and Val," Mary recognized that she didn't say Mommy, "that I'm a *polyploid,* or more specifically, a tetraploid. And Jon might be too."

"What's a polyploid?" Chris asked.

"Well," Mary took a deep breath. "It's complicated. But it means we have different chromosomes. More of them. And polyploid humans have never existed before, according to Dr. Walt."

"Polyploid," Jon said, letting it sink in. "Yes, that makes sense." His voice overpowered the room. His accent was Cajun like his mother's, and Mary loved it. "Yes," he continued, "I've always thought there was a genetic cause for how I am. I've read everything I could get my hands on about gigantism, but nothing fits. I'm normal, not deformed, which is how giants are usually described. And you seem normal to me too, Mary."

Mary's face flushed. She could feel her heart pounding. This was chemistry for sure. He looked into her eyes, and Mary realized he was waiting for her response. Finally managing to gain some control, she said, "Polyploidy explains everything about us. Val described to me the effects of polyploidy in plants, her specialty. She said polyploid plants are much more vigorous: taller, mature earlier, and withstand droughts and poor soil. Of course, the soil and drought parts don't apply to us."

Jon laughed, contagiously, then Mary too. She continued, "Polyploid races in animals are also more robust and vigorous than normal."

"If there are no other primate polyploids, then we're the first," Jon said. "How did it happen? Why now and not before?"

Mary was impressed that he already knew about polyploidy, and that he had been working on why he was the way he was. "Walt thinks we were artificially made through genetic engineering, probably by my father, Dr. Solven. Walt wants to see if you're polyploid too, Jon. And he needs to see your sex chromosomes."

"That makes sense. If I were XXXY, I would be intersexual, right? Did he talk about that?" Jon asked.

He could be smarter than I am, Mary thought. "You understand this already, Jon. Yes, he talked about diploid humans with XXY being intersexual. Even if you're XXYY, he's not sure that you are fertile. Furthermore, XXXX's like me might not be fertile," Mary said. She felt herself blushing and began to rock her chair.

"Now, I understand what Dr. Solven meant," Chris said. "He mentioned a race of superhumans and even talked about how it would change everything. I thought he was writing a science fiction novel. His English wasn't always clear to me."

"What's he like?" Mary said. "I've never seen him. Well, not since I was a baby."

"I don't like him much, at least not now. I liked him well enough at first. But he used me to make a baby for his super race," Chris said. "I love my baby, but it's been hard for us, hasn't it, Jon? And what concern did he really have about your future? He didn't even bother to tell us parents what was going on until it was too late."

She was staring at Mary. "Tell Val to call me. The other parents want to meet."

"Others?"

"Yes. You have relatives, you might say. I'll explain everything to Val. The sooner the better."

XXXX

Parents and their giant children began to gather in the auditorium-style classroom. Val, David, Mary, Chris, Jon, and the others. Mary and Jon greeted each other like old friends. They laughed when they tried to squeeze into the too-small desks in the front corner of the classroom. They gave up and sat on the floor, leaning against a sidewall where they could see the others.

Val was stunned by the children's extraordinary height and attractiveness. They were racially diverse—African-American, white and brown-skinned, Mideastern, Hispanic, Asian. They could have been from anywhere, and seemed to have come from nowhere. They had uniformly lean and seemingly unblemished bodies. They were as perfect looking as robots, almost inhuman, yet they spoke like children. Human children. How could polyploidy alone induce such perfection? She remembered the magnificent polyploids of *Eupatorium*, in the plant kingdom, that towered over the puny diploids in mixed populations.

Parents sat in the classroom desks. Children sat on the floor, scattered along the aisles and walls of the room.

Val said, "Thanks for coming on such short notice. Sorry about the seating. I hope you'll be comfortable enough."

There were murmurings of agreement or happiness. She couldn't tell which.

"We are here tonight through the efforts of Chris Landry. She has courageously introduced herself to many of you, whose children are like her son, Jon. I, too, am overwhelmed and pleased that you decided to come tonight. I thought my Mary was unique. Now I see she's one of you."

Val held up a pad and pen and handed it to a nearby woman.

"Please write down your contact information and pass the pad and pen on to the family nearest you. I'll compile the information and share it with all of you. If you have email, please include that address."

She took a deep breath. "I have some information that is very important. Dr. Walter Klein, a scientist at Vermilion State University, examined Mary's karyotype, the number and size of each of her chromosomes." She pointed to Mary, who waved. "And Dr. Klein discovered that Mary is polyploid, like possibly many of you." She let that rest a second. "That means, in the simplest of terms, that your chromosomes aren't like the rest of the human race."

Several parents called out, "Polyploids? What does that mean?"

"Good question. In short, they have double our number of chromosomes. But before we get too caught up in technicalities, I'd like to ask a few questions that will help us determine if your children are polyploid."

No one spoke.

"How many of you used the Solven Fertility Clinic to conceive?"

Most, perhaps all, the women raised their hands.

"That seems to be everyone who looks like a mother," Val said.

Someone laughed, easing the tension.

"A question for the children. How old are you? Wait! Raise your hands when I call your age. I'll write the totals on the board."

Mary stood and said, "I'll count for you, Val."

Val called out ages. No hands went up until she reached six. At eight, no one raised a hand.

"No one older?" The kids shook their heads. "Then the ages of the children here tonight are six and seven, which suggests all of you went to the Solven Clinic during the two years it was operating in town. And," she glanced at the board, "at least thirty-two children were conceived with the help of the Solven Clinic."

"Did any mother have prenatal care at a place other than Solven's?" No one raised a hand.

"Are there any mothers whose children were born in a hospital other than Solven's?"

The room was quiet.

"OK. Solven's seems to have been a full service facility. One more question. Do you think your child is exceptional?"

Hands went up. Val felt goose bumps on her arms, and she saw a few parents crying.

Then someone rushed toward the front of the room. He shoved Mary against the blackboard on the back wall. He shouted, "How fabulous that we found out that dear Dr. Solven made us freaks. Do we want another one like him, another Solven, messing with our lives? I don't intend to take anymore crap from another doctor, or scientist, or whatever this woman is."

"Michael, please sit down," a woman called from a back row. "We don't want trouble."

Michael said, "I'm running this meeting now, so don't speak until I recognize you. Comments? Questions? Mary, go snuggle with your boyfriend."

Michael's muscles bulged through his tight pink T-shirt, and he looked even taller than Jon. Val dialed campus security, then stopped, realizing Michael would overwhelm them, and there would be more trouble.

"Michael," she tried another tact, "you're angry. But shouldn't we all decide?"

"No, I decide, just like you did. We didn't vote you in. And we don't want Solven's daughter keeping tabs on us." He grinned, brushing his dark hair from his eyes.

Val realized she had no idea how to deal with him.

Michael's father stood. One of his eyes was swollen, and his neck was bruised. "Michael Pitre, you have to let these people continue with their meeting. Let's go home. You're out of control."

Michael didn't move. "I'm not finished, and I'm in charge here."

Val stepped toward Michael, and he shoved her. Jon and a few others jumped up and converged on Michael, pinning him to the floor.

"Let me up, you monsters."

"What's wrong with you?" Jon said.

Michael twisted and turned, but his superior strength wasn't enough to overcome so many.

"OK, OK. If you turn me loose, I'll go peacefully. Just let me go."

He leaped up and ran from the room, clambering over the children seated on the floor.

Mr. Pitre stood and said apologetically, "We hoped to get some help with Michael when we came here, and I guess we have. The rest of you don't act like him. Father Landry at St. Joseph's couldn't help us either."

"He needs medication," someone said. "He's bipolar or schizophrenic. He needs help."

It was unclear what was happening.

Then Chris raised her hand. "How do we find out if our children are polyploid?"

"I can help with that," Walt said from the back of the room. "From what I've seen of the other children here, I'd say there's a high probability that they're polyploid. But I'd like to be sure." He brushed his curly red hair away from his eyes.

"All I need is a small blood sample. I think every child here could be a polyploid. We already know about Mary. Let's do this. Come to my lab, and I'll test them. I can assure you no harm will come to your children."

Mr. Pitre said, "Before you all get carried away, I have something else to say. We all love our children, but not when they're not like us. What Dr. Solven did was wrong. He was trying to create something unnatural. It's malpractice. All of us were part of his experiment, weren't we? And he's probably still doing it somewhere else. I say we find him and set this straight!"

XXYY

The following morning, Val, Mary, and Jon arrived at George H. Bush International Airport in Houston. Mary and Jon had attracted considerable interest. Val had responded to strange looks by explaining that she was a basketball coach, that Mary and Jon were players. Val had told Dr. Solven she was bringing Mary, but she hadn't mentioned Jon. Mary had insisted that Jon come with them.

When they arrived, Jon programmed the GPS in their rental car for the Solven Fertility Clinic, 1302 St. Mark's Parkway. Val noticed how at ease he was. He had found their airline gate, helped with directions, and handled other logistics that usually irritated Val, a seasoned traveler.

The Solven Clinic building was a rambling, one-story structure with red tile roof and white stucco exterior, typical Houston architecture. Val parked near the front entrance. Inside, the waiting room was crowded with pregnant women accompanied by nervous-looking men They all stared openly at Mary and Jon.

Val gave her name and Mary's to Dr. Solven's receptionist through a hole in the sliding glass window. "Sign the register, please," the receptionist said noncommittally.

A plump woman in nurse's white opened the door. "Dr. Smythe and Mary, Dr. Solven will see you now." Mary motioned Jon to follow. Unlike those in the waiting room, the nurse seemed to have little interest in them. "This way, please." She indicated a wide hallway with paintings of children and mothers on the walls. In an old style courtliness, Jon indicated that they should go ahead of him. Val wondered where he'd learned that behavior.

Dr. Solven rose from behind his broad, antique-looking mahogany desk and smiled. His handsome face was framed by hair so light that it appeared silver. Judging from his growing middle, Val guessed he was fairly out of shape, in his mid-forties. Unlike his offspring, he was of average height, but his intense blue eyes mirrored Mary's. He went to Mary and hugged her. Then he began speaking to her in Russian.

At first Val thought Mary appeared shaken by his affectionate hug, but in response to hearing her mother's tongue, any wariness at meeting her absentee father seemed to disappear.

Their conversation continued in Russian for a while, then Val heard her name among the Russian words, and Dr. Solven turned to her and reached out to shake her hand. Then Mary introduced Jon in Russian, and Dr. Solven stepped forward and hugged him, as if he too, like Mary, was his child.

Val, feeling excluded, said, "Mary, could you and your father please speak English?"

"I'm so sorry, Dr. Smythe," Dr. Solven said, "We're being impolite. I don't have many opportunities to speak Russian." His English was surprisingly clear, but not entirely easy to understand. He thanked Val for taking Mary in after Erika's death. "She has developed nicely, and so has Jon. I don't usually get to meet my children after they're born. My plan was to check in on them after they had matured."

Val interrupted. "That's what we came to talk to you about. Your children, as you call them, are polyploid. How did you engineer this and why?"

She expected his denial or apology. What she heard was, "I'm saving humankind." He paused and smiled easily. "Can't you see? You're a biologist. So you know that multiplying the DNA gives more potential for evolution. Look at the two specimens here." He leaned back against his desk. "Why wait for the slow steps of evolution when we have all the genes we need scattered about in other creatures?

"The multiplication of genes in polyploidy provides a safe new substrate for evolution to work. Normal humans are headed for extinction. We all know that. We have a big load of bad genes we're passing down to our children. So I carefully selected parents, or if you prefer, genes, for my children. Philosophers and religious figures have written about superhumans for a long time, and now I've created that super-race. Now we wait to see if they can reproduce." He turned to Mary and Jon. "Have you started your periods, Mary? And Jon, do you have wet dreams?"

They blushed and answered yes. Val was stunned by his forwardness.

"Good, good. Things are working as planned. I spliced in genes from other species to improve your genomes. Like most other animals, my children can make vitamin C because they have genes extracted from the slow loris, a primate species. Cancer will never kill them, and common colds will never make them sick."

"So you subscribe to the ideas of Linus Pauling about Vitamin C?" Val said.

"Of course. My children also have genes for parthenogenesis from a nematode, *Caenorhabditis elegans*, and the means of regeneration from the planarian flatworm. We've created transgenic polyploid humans with genes harvested from other organisms. No doubt you realize what this means, Dr. Smythe?"

Val wasn't sure what to say. Initially, she had marveled at how brilliantly he had solved so many complex genetic problems, and who knows, maybe he had improved the human race. But he also ignored the social consequences, the ethics of what he was conjuring. Using parents for his experiment without their consent or knowledge was monstrous. She tried to respond scientifically. "I can see splicing in genes for regeneration, and perhaps the dubious vitamin C, but not parthenogenesis. That's absurd!"

"Perhaps, Dr. Smythe, the parthenogenesis genes may not

work. We'll have to see. But if the children can reproduce, even if only by cloning, well…"

Val continued, "The hubris to carry out such experiments is incredible. You've violated your oath as a physician and opened yourself to malpractice suits." She looked at Mary and Jon who stood silently. How did they feel about being the product of an experiment? Normal humans wouldn't accept them once they knew what they were. "Didn't you think about what their lives would be like? Racial discrimination is nothing compared to what Mary, Jon, and others like them will experience."

"But they'll win the battles. I've thought of everything; they're prepared. The only feature of my transgenic polyploid humans that I hadn't expected is their exceptional intelligence. Imagine the problems they can solve for themselves. Normal diploid humans will need them. You'll see."

"Normal?" Val asked. "Is that a good word to use?" In their presence? Val glanced at the children and shifted uncomfortably.

Mary broke the silence. "We know we're not normal in the sense he means. I'm not offended. Are you, Jon? I understand what he's tried to do. I'm curious about his motivation, but it's up to us to make our lives meaningful."

Jon squeezed Mary's hand. Being in love was meaning enough for them, Val thought.

"Do I see a little romance developing between you two?" Dr. Solven said. "Marvelous! How would you like to stay in Houston for a few days? There's much to see and do: the aquarium, IMAX, art museums, libraries, movies, and excellent restaurants. How about it? I could have my receptionist reschedule your flight for next week."

"You and Jon aren't prepared to stay in Houston, Mary," Val objected. "You didn't bring enough clothes. You should plan to come back another time."

"By the way, Dr. Smythe, I've compiled a manuscript of notes on the methods and techniques I used to create my children. It's locked away in my safe. I plan to publish it when I know the end of the story."

"What do you mean by the end of the story?" Val asked.

"You'll see, Dr. Smythe," he said. "Very soon."

Mary wanted to stay with her father. Jon called to tell his mother he was also staying in Houston. Val drove back to the airport, early and alone.

CHAPTER 5

Mary's father treated them to lunch at a restaurant serving Russian food. Over lunch and in her parent's native tongue, Mary asked her father many of the questions she had accumulated: Where had he grown up in Russia? When had he come to the U. S.? Where had he attended medical school? And how had he met her mother? She couldn't bring herself to ask why he had abandoned them.

Mary was mesmerized, and she had almost forgotten about Jon, until he spoke to her in clear, if simple, Russian.

"Jon, I didn't know you spoke Russian," Mary said.

"After two hours of nonstop listening, I think I could pick up any language. Besides," Jon continued in English, "I want to know everything about you. Russian is a part of you, your native language."

Interrupting them, Dr. Solven turned to Jon, "Mary said you were interested in studying medicine. Maybe I can help."

"Yes, but my age and education are problems. I don't even have a high school diploma. Val's husband, David, has offered to forge new documents for us. Of course, Mary has the same problems."

"I think Tom Bradford can help, Jon. He's a gynecologist specializing in prenatal care here at the clinic. He knows all about my work. Maybe he can do a little postnatal care," he said, laughing.

Dr. Solven phoned Bradford while they ate.

"Tom has time to see you in an hour, Jon. His office is down the hall from mine."

As they walked back to the clinic after lunch, Dr. Solven made another call, then outlined a plan for their stay in Houston. "Tomorrow I work at the clinic, and over the weekend I'm on call in obstetrics. You two will be on your own for a few days, so I've arranged for my driver, Bob Nelson, to take you wherever you want to go. I gave him a list of places I think you'll like. After Jon's meeting with Tom, I suggest you buy clothes and things you'll need for the week. Mary, remind me to give you my credit card when we get to the clinic."

Mary waited for Jon in her father's office. To her delight, Dr. Solven talked to her about Russia. Jon returned an hour later looking pleased.

He was about to speak when Dr. Solven said, "Later I want to hear all about your conversation with Tom, Jon. But for now, you and Mary need to go shopping. Your driver is waiting."

Mary felt like Russian royalty with her Prince Jon, a carriage, and driver. Dr. Solven introduced Bob and instructed him to take them to the Galleria mall. Bob dropped them at the mall entrance, saying he'd run a few errands and meet them in an hour.

The Galleria, a city within the city of Houston, was crowded with shoppers, and like the children they were, Mary and Jon were dazzled by everything—the tightly packed moving throngs of people, the architecture, glass atria, and sheer size of the mall. The magnificent structure, built of various types of stone and wood, had suspended glass balconies and skylights, and it was furnished with plush leather sofas and chairs for tired shoppers. They passed Neiman Marcus, Cartier, Gucci, Tiffany & Co., none of which they knew. Mary suggested they find Dillard's, where she had shopped with her mother. She knew they stocked both men's and women's clothing.

As they searched the mall for the store they wanted, they realized that people were staring at them, and a few teenagers trailed along behind them.

"We're attracting too much attention. Let's sit," Mary suggested, hoping their followers would become bored and leave. Mary pointed to an empty table in the food court. "I'll get us some orange juice. With only one of us standing, we won't be so noticeable. Then I want to hear about your conversation with Dr. Bradford."

When she returned with their drinks, she found that their followers were talking with Jon about basketball. He pretended to be a new recruit for the Houston Rockets. Fortunately, he seemed to know about the game and teams and was obviously convincing.

"Is she a basketball star, too?" one of the boys asked.

"Yes, she plays for the Lady Tigers of LSU," Jon answered, smiling at Mary. "She doesn't speak English very well. She's Russian." Mary nodded, turned away, and said something in Russian. Jon had given her a good excuse not to speak. Faking English with a Russian accent might be tricky. Also, all the basketball she knew was from that pickup game in Gerald Park.

Eventually, satisfied and bored, the teenagers drifted away. Jon and Mary resumed their trip to Dillard's, using a map of the mall they had picked up at the food court. Jon held Mary's hand and told her about his meeting with Dr. Bradford.

"He said I should get a fake ID giving my age as eighteen and take the GED. Since I'm a Louisiana resident, he said to take the test there as soon as possible. He questioned me about what I'd read, and he said that with my knowledge I could test out of most of the college courses required for a bachelor's degree. He wants me to call him about med-school when I get my bachelor's degree."

"You can order forms for the GED online while we're here," Mary said. "My dad, I mean Dr. Solven, probably has a computer at home."

"Mary, you should take the GED with me," Jon said.

"Yeah, let's call David now and tell him to make our ages eighteen on the new birth certificates," Mary said. "No, wait, there's Dillard's."

Mary bought several pairs of pants and jeans, which were capri length on her, and blouses and pajamas in the largest size she could find. She modeled the clothes for Jon as if they were a young married couple. She selected subdued colors to attract less attention. Her mother had always insisted on buying clothes no one would notice.

"Are you basketball players?" asked the clerk waiting on Mary.

"Yes, we are."

"It's wonderful to have common interests," the clerk said, smiling pleasantly.

In Dillard's, Jon found underwear large enough, but no pants to fit him. The clerk suggested a specialty store. Mary paid with her father's credit card.

On the way to the specialty store, they saw an enormous man in a dirty pink T-shirt walking in their direction on the opposite side of the corridor. "Jon, look, that's Michael Pitre. Hey, Michael," Mary called as they approached him.

Michael stopped, and then suddenly ran in the opposite direction.

"Why did he run away?" Mary said.

"I guess he's angry about being wrestled down at the meeting," Jon said.

The specialty store had shirts that were wide enough in the shoulders, but their pants were too short. Mary liked the way he looked in the khaki, cargo shorts, and collared navy blue knit shirt. He picked up several other pairs of shorts and collared shirts in subdued colors, although he was drawn to the brighter tones.

Mary's cell phone rang. Val. Mary told her about seeing Michael at the Galleria, still in his pink shirt. Val warned her to stay away from him, and she'd tell the Pitres that he was in Houston.

"Dr. Solven is being so nice to us. After we finish shopping, we have dinner reservations, and tomorrow we go sightseeing." ... "No, he isn't with us right now. He's working." ... "Bob is driving us around." ... "I guess we'll see him at dinner." ... "No, I don't think he's up to anything."

Bob was waiting for them near the mall entrance. "Dr. Solven called to say he made reservations for seven-thirty at Damian's Cucina Italian, a fine dining restaurant not far from the Galleria. Also, he won't be joining you for dinner."

As they were driving out of the Galleria parking lot, they saw Michael again. "See that guy in the pink shirt, Bob? Could you get close enough for us to talk to him?"

"That giant?" Bob headed toward Michael.

But Michael saw their SUV and jumped into a black van parked nearby. He revved the engine and squealed out of the parking lot.

"What did you do to him?" Bob asked.

"Just an old grudge. We thought we could make amends, but he doesn't want to," Mary said. She wondered if Michael was in

Houston because his parents had kicked him out.

Bob dropped them off and said he'd eat at McDonald's and wait out front. When they protested, he insisted that Dr. Solven had said the restaurant would be crowded. "Not enough room in the inn," he joked, and he was fine with McDonald's; simple tastes for a simple man.

Damian's Cucina Italian was crowded, but the maître d' seated them in a quiet corner and brought a bottle of Sauvignon Blanc that Dr. Solven had ordered. He had also ordered their food.

Murals of Italian mountain scenes, vineyards, and peasants covered the restaurant walls. Philodendron vines draped over the arched doorways and window ledges. The pleasant spicy scent of food and the yeasty smell of fresh bread piqued their appetites.

Mary sipped her wine, the first she'd ever tasted. Looking at Jon, she thought him the handsomest man in the universe. He smiled, reaching for her hand.

A waiter dressed in black pants and crisp white shirt brought the antipasti. "Appetizers for you: *Prosciutto con Asparagi*, prosciutto and steamed asparagus with a lemon vinaigrette and *Insalata Naparst*, a selection of fresh seafood tossed with tomato, onion, olives, ricotta cheese, extra virgin olive oil, lemon, and herbs. Enjoy."

The amount of food made them laugh. "If these are the appetizers, how big are their entrées?" Jon laughed, and they ate heartily, sharing their food.

The waiter appeared as they were finishing their antipasti. He poured them more wine and cleared their antipasti plates. Quickly he returned from the kitchen with their entrées. "For you *signorina*, we have *Eggplant Parmigiana*, baked eggplant with mozzarella cheese, fresh tomato sauce, and basil. For you *signore*, we have *Veal Piccata*, veal sautéed with lemon, fresh parsley, and a white wine butter. Is there anything else?"

"I think that's all we need. Thank you," Jon said.

After clearing the entrée plates, the waiter brought desserts. The *Tre Latte* he described as a white chocolate espresso cake soaked in three sweet milks with Kahlua whipping cream, and *Tiramisu*, as layers of sweetened, rum-flavored mascarpone cheese, chocolate, and ladyfingers flavored with espresso. "Does my father want to fatten us up or just see how much taller we'll grow?" They shared desserts back and forth until their plates were clean.

By the time she paid the bill, Mary felt tipsy and more than a little amorous. Without thinking, Mary said, "I love you," and remembered the chemistry of love that Val had warned her about. So what? *I want to enjoy this moment.*

"I love you too, Mary."

Bob was waiting for them outside. Mary climbed into the front seat, and Jon sat in back as before. She wanted to sit next to Jon and put her head on his shoulder, but there wasn't enough room for both of them in the backseat. She fell asleep, waking as Bob turned into a private drive off River Oaks Boulevard. He pressed a remote to open a black wrought iron gate. Inside the tall, white stucco wall surrounding the grounds, the headlights beamed on an enormous Spanish style house of stucco with a red gabled roof. Palms, bird of paradise plants, carefully groomed shrubbery, and beds of annual flowers embellished the home.

Bob parked in the garage, and Mary and Jon unloaded their bags of new clothes. Bob unlocked the door and said that Dr. Solven would be staying in his clinic apartment. He explained that Sonia would prepare breakfast by eight, and he'd be back at ten to take them sightseeing. Then he left.

Mary and Jon looked at each other.

"Wow. Let's look around."

There were five bedrooms, each with its own bath. The kitchen contained more appliances and hanging cookware than Mary had ever seen. An eating nook overlooked a lighted backyard, and French doors opened to a pool. In the dining room, a formal table seated sixteen. And glass-fronted cabinets in two corners showcased crystal glassware and china. Mary recognized the china pattern as her mother's and felt tears swelling.

Mary resented that her mother hadn't lived nearly as well as her father. Why was he suddenly being generous now? Perhaps Val should be suspicious.

She reached for Jon's hand, and he pulled her to him. She met his lips for the first romantic kiss of her life. Thoughts abandoned her, and feelings mingled intricately with physical sensations. His lips were soft even as his body was muscled and taut against her.

She felt out of control and didn't care.

XXXX

Mary was startled awake by bright sunlight streaming through the bedroom window. Finding herself naked beside Jon, she smiled, remembering the wonderful night. She touched his shoulder, and he opened his eyes. *"Bonjour, chère,"* he said in his Cajun French.

"Jon, we have to get dressed. I hear Sonia in the kitchen. Go to another bedroom, quickly."

Jon gathered up the bags of new clothes along with the clothes he'd removed the night before. Mary watched, admiring his perfect body. She never wanted to be separated from him again, even by the walls of this house. She got out of bed and pressed herself against his bare back, enjoying the pleasure of his skin against hers. She kissed his shoulders. He turned sideways to kiss her lips. Reluctantly, she pulled away, and he left the room.

Promptly at eight, Sonia, whose dark skin glowed beautifully in the morning light, served them breakfast. She only spoke Spanish and didn't try to talk with them. But she smiled, and they felt as comfortable as if they'd known her all their lives. The scrambled eggs, bacon, whole-wheat toast, fresh orange juice, and coffee tasted delicious. And Mary doctored her coffee lavishly with cream and sugar, all the while hearing her mother's admonition that she was too young to drink coffee. What would she have said about last night with Jon? Everything was happening so quickly.

Jon looked into Mary's eyes. "I love you, Mary. We're meant to be together. It feels right and wonderful. Will you marry me?"

"Jon, I'm six years old and you're seven. They won't let us."

"We're getting new birth certificates, Mary. No one will know how old we really are."

She stood, not knowing, yet knowing, what she'd say. "Yes. I mean…"

Jon opened the wide French doors and looked out at the pool. "Let's go for a swim before Bob gets here."

"I don't have a bathing suit." Mary said.

"We don't need them do we, *chère*?" he said, grinning like a teenager, as if that was what he'd suddenly become.

Mary stripped off her pajamas, and Jon removed his new navy T-shirt, khaki shorts, and briefs at the pool's edge. The high stucco fence secluded them from the neighbors, and they didn't notice when Sonia came to the doorway and smiled.

XXYY

They were waiting in the living room when Bob arrived with a package. Handing it to Mary, he said, "He wanted you to have this."

Mary opened it, finding a typed manuscript and sealed envelope addressed to her. Before opening the letter, she glanced at the title, *The New Humans,* by Dr. Maximilian Solven. Mary ripped open the envelope. The letter inside was typed on clinic letterhead.

Dear Mary,

I know I haven't been the best of fathers, but I consider you the product of my mind. You and the others are a superior race and will save humans from extinction. In the manuscript, you'll find an explanation of the techniques that I used to make you and the others. Mankind will thank me for this someday. But until then, you must lead this new race of humans. I am a diploid human and cannot provide that leadership, or even imagine how you must feel with all your exceptional powers and abilities. The leader must be one of you. Along with techniques and methods in the manuscript, you'll find the names and addresses of all my polyploid children. I suggest that you begin communicating with these disparate groups. They need to understand who they are.

Please keep this manuscript out of public hands, but use the information in it to help the polyploid race understand its biology. There is still much to learn because the oldest of you is only fifteen years old and lives in North Korea. You have genes for healing and repair through regeneration and for parthenogenesis.

There is much to learn about polyploid biology and development; two of the most important are: Can you reproduce? And how will the parthenogenesis genes work in humans?

I'll be in contact with you after you leave Houston. In the meantime, learn from the manuscript. Someday you'll inherit everything else I have, as well. Use it for the betterment of mankind.

Best of luck,

Max, your father

Mary handed the letter to Jon and sat down in the red leather chair in the living room to scan the manuscript. She handed pages to Jon, who read them quickly.

Bob said, "Dr. Solven suggested that I take you all to the Natural History Museum and then to the NASA Space Center. The IMAX at the museum has a show called *Sharks 3D*. For tonight, he bought tickets for the Hobby Center for you to see *Fiddler on the Roof.*"

"Wow. Thanks, Bob, but we want to read this before we go anywhere," Mary said, pointing to the manuscript.

"No problem, I'll gas up and be back in a half hour. Does that give you enough time?"

They read. "What an amazing feat of genetic engineering!" Jon said. They commented back and forth, and Mary realized that he was as interesting intellectually as he was physically. Val would approve of this chemistry, wouldn't she?

"How did he expect us to function in a diploid society? As polyploids, we can't mate with them, and they won't accept us when they know what we are," Mary said.

"He lacks normal human emotions, if you ask me. Look at what he did to his own family," Jon said.

Bob returned, and they squeezed into the SUV for the short ride downtown. As they were leaving the neighborhood and nearing the road leading into the city, a black van sped past them.

"That looks like Michael's van. What would he be doing in this neighborhood? Please follow it, Bob. If it is Michael, I want to talk to him," Mary said.

Bob turned the SUV around in a driveway and followed the van. They watched as it stopped in front of Dr. Solven's house.

Michael left the van and walked toward the house.

"Let's talk to him," Mary said, as Bob pulled in beside Michael's van.

Michael was pounding on the door when he heard Jon and Mary behind him.

"What are you doing here?" Michael asked. "Oh yeah, Mary's visiting her papa. Where's the good doctor? Ha, ha."

"Would you like to come in, Michael? Have you had breakfast?" Mary said.

Michael reeked of unwashed stench, and she didn't relish being any closer to him. She wondered if he had bathed since the meeting over a week ago. He obviously had not changed his pink T-shirt.

"No, I don't want any damn breakfast, freaks. I want to make Solven pay for what he's done and stop him from creating any more freaks like us."

"He's not here, Michael... and we don't know where he is." Mary hoped her expression didn't betray her lie. "What do you mean by wanting him to pay? Let's go inside and talk."

"He's at the clinic, isn't he?" Michael tossed his head to the side, flinging a thick strand of greasy black hair away from his eyes. The front of his pink shirt was stained with food, and sweat ringed his underarms. He turned abruptly, walked back to the black van, and peeled out, leaving the sulfur smell of burnt tires.

Mary could see the worry in the faces of Bob and Jon. "We need to get to the clinic as fast as possible," Mary said.

Bob flipped his phone open. Mary and Jon listened to him explain to Dr. Solven that his life was in danger from a gigantic man named Michael.

"You can't reason with this man. He has crazy eyes, and he's out to get you," Bob said. "I'm calling the police, right now." ... "What? You're not talking me out of it." ... "Fire me, then."

"Please let me talk to him," Mary said, reaching for the phone.

While Mary was talking to her father, they all got into the SUV, and Bob sped toward the clinic.

"He's afraid calling the police could make trouble for us," Mary said. "And he doesn't want any publicity. He said it would be detrimental to his plan. I wonder what he means by that.'"

"I can't handle him by myself," Jon spoke up. "And the police can't either. Unless they try to kill him."

XXXX

They saw Michael's van in front of the clinic and hurried inside. Bob nodded to the receptionist, who knew him, and knocked once before pushing open the door to Dr. Solven's office. He lay on the floor. Michael looked up from behind the desk where he was rifling through the file drawers.

Mary rushed to her father, pressing her fingers against his bruised, twisted neck. "Michael. What have you done? He's dead."

"Yeah, we're rid of this curse of a human." Michael laughed maniacally. "Now I've got to find his notebooks. He kept records. They all do. Those other doctors making freaks too. I have to stop them." He went to a filing cabinet. Mary noticed the deep, bleeding scratches on his neck, as he continued his chaotic search, opening doors, rummaging through files, muttering to himself about doctors making freaks.

Mary reached for the phone on the desk. But Michael anticipated and grabbed her hand, forcing her to drop the phone, which broke when it hit the floor. Jon who had been trying to revive Dr. Solven, flung himself against Michael, knocking him away from Mary. Michael started to lose his balance, then turned nimbly, and with a sweep of his arm sent Jon sprawling.

Mary and Bob went for Michael, but he threw Bob as if he were little more than an afterthought. Several plaques crashed to the floor as Bob fell across the desk. Then both Mary and Jon lunged for Michael, who was too quick, dashing from the room.

The noise had brought other clinic staff to investigate, but Michael brushed them aside as he hurried from the office. Mary went to Bob and, checking his carotid, found a pulse. "He's alive, but he needs help. Call the police."

CHAPTER 5

XXYY

"How long have you been doing forgeries, David?" Val asked. They were sitting at the glass top table eating one of David's sumptuous Saturday breakfasts. "Have I been living with a criminal?"

"It's a long story. As a priest, I did charity work with indigent Mexican people along the border. Poverty is a way of life for those people. Their only chance is to make money in America to send home to their families. I've continued that work ever since. If you had known, you'd be culpable under the law. Am I a criminal for helping poor Hispanic people live a better life? I don't think so."

Val could think of nothing else to say and silently, reasoning to herself, ate breakfast. David was involved in illegal activity, but he was a good man. Still, he'd concealed his forgeries from her. But she had to admit she was pleased he was helping Mary.

"Have any of the children from the meeting asked you to forge documents for them, David?"

"Yes. Just about every one of them, including that crazy boy, Michael. He seemed so threatening, I did it to get rid of him."

"How did he threaten you?"

"He huffed around, paced, and looked crazy, as if he was on a short fuse. He's a big guy. I wanted to avoid trouble."

XXXX

Two Hispanic officers, neatly dressed and showing Houston Police Department badges arrived within minutes. Detective Juan Rodriguez's tanned face was marred by a recent scar that ran from his chin to just below his eye. His partner put on latex gloves and bent to examine Dr. Solven's body, as Rodriguez called for assistance.

"The killer can't be too far away," Mary said. "He's driving a black van. He's tall, taller than we are. His name is Michael

Pitre."

"How do you know he's driving a black van if you're in here?" Detective Rodriguez wrote something on his small flip pad. "And taller than you are? That would make him one hell of a pro basketball prospect. Yeah, right." He stared up at Mary and Jon. "What are the chances of finding two giants in one place, let alone three?"

"We know Michael from Vermilion, Louisiana, where we live. Jon and I are staying with my father, Dr. Maximilian Solven, and Michael followed us here. We were all conceived at my father's fertility clinic when he practiced in Vermilion. Michael didn't like being a giant, or freak as he called it, and he wanted to get even with my father for creating us," Mary tried to explain.

"Are you saying that another giant killed this man?" Rodriguez smirked. "And he's your father? Sounds like a fairy tale to me."

A second police team had arrived by now, and Bob was sitting up, holding a cold cloth on his forehead. Rodriguez looked at Bob. "What's your story, shorty?"

"My story is the same as hers," Bob said, cocking his head toward Mary.

"And you? Jon, is it?"

"Mary's telling the truth. Don't you want to know how he was killed?" Jon asked.

"Well, yeah. Did you see this other giant do it?"

"No, we didn't, but he was in the office when we got here. Dr. Solven lay on the floor dead, and Michael was searching through his files." Jon described his fight with Michael.

"What was this other giant looking for?"

Mary's cheeks felt hot. "Why aren't you searching for Michael? He killed my father and admitted it to us. The longer you delay, the farther he'll be from here."

"Don't worry about that. We alerted the station. If he comes close to one of our cars, he's toast."

"You'll need extra help. He's very strong. It took two others like me to restrain him at a meeting," Jon said.

"You giants held a meeting? Not about basketball either, right? This story gets more interesting all the time," Rodriguez said.

Mary realized they'd volunteered too much information. The

part of the story they had told Rodriguez about themselves did seem preposterous. And the more they revealed, the more trouble they'd be in.

"Do you need me anymore? I need to tell my mother what's happened." Mary wanted to ask Val what they should do.

"Where does she live?" Rodriguez asked.

"In Vermilion, Louisiana," Mary said.

"This doctor's wife lives in Vermilion?"

"No, she's my stepmother. My mother is dead."

"How did she die?"

"From cancer."

"Is this woman your father's second wife?"

"Actually she's not really my stepmother, I just call her that. My mother appointed her my guardian. She was our neighbor in Vermilion. She's a biologist at the university."

"Why would you need a guardian?"

"I, I'm," Mary stammered, almost revealing her age, before catching herself. When would this quagmire of detail stop getting her in trouble? She looked at Jon, whose blank stare advised her to say as little as possible.

"You're what? Out with it! Or we can all go down to the station for a discussion," Rodriguez said.

"My mother thought I needed an advisor. At the time, my father was out of the picture," Mary lied. "He left us after I was born. He seemed eager to see me after my mother died. That's why I flew to Houston."

"You haven't seen him since he left you and your mother?"

"No," Mary said, trying to shorten her answers.

"I get the feeling you're withholding information." Rodriguez made a few more notes. "Did Jon come to Houston with you?"

"Yes, we flew here together."

"When did you arrive in Houston?"

"Two days ago."

"Where are you staying?"

"At my father's house."

"How do you know this pair, Bob?"

"I'm their driver."

"Can't they drive?"

"No, they are... They don't know the city, so Dr. Solven asked me to drive them around sightseeing. I work for him or, that is, did work for him."

"Let me see your driver's licenses." Bob handed Rodriguez his, and the detective copied some information. Mary looked at Jon and saw the same anxiety she felt.

"I'm sorry officer," Jon said. "We don't have IDs with us."

Rodriguez glowered. "Give me your full names and addresses. I suggest you go straight home." He turned to Bob. "And if you're driving them, make sure they get there and stay until I get back in touch. You're not under arrest yet, but I know you're not telling me everything, and I'll get to the bottom of this. I wouldn't want to be in your shoes," he took in their sizes again, "if you're lying to me."

CHAPTER 6

"We can't leave Houston," Mary told Val as Bob drove them back to Dr. Solven's house. "What if they find out we're polyploids? We'll be in even more trouble."

"I'll be there as soon as I can get a flight."

When they arrived at Dr. Solven's house, Bob unlocked the door and led them inside.

"I work for you now, Mary," Bob said. "Whatever you want me to do, I'm here for you. I know that's what your father would have wanted. And I want to find the bastard that killed him... He told me his special children would save mankind, and I believe him." He paused, took a deep breath. "But right now, I'm beat, and my head hurts. I'm going home, but you'll be safe from Michael here. Your father had quite a burglar alarm system installed. And I wouldn't be surprised if the car I see out front isn't the police watching the neighborhood. But if you need me, call. I'll see you in the morning."

She hugged him, and a feeling rushed through her. Her arms still around him, she realized she was stronger physically than he was. Yet he felt secure, like a father.

"Yes," she said. "See you in the morning."

XXYY

"*The New Humans*. My, what a title!" Val said, accepting the manuscript from Mary. "I guess you've both read this already? Of course, what a silly question." She smiled at them. "I'm tired from the flight, but I want to have a look at this now. There must be a bottle of wine in this mansion somewhere. I can't imagine Dr. Solven didn't have a wine cellar."

"Yes, there's wine in the refrigerator—Pinot Grigio," Mary

said.

"I'll find glasses," Jon said.

Val considered that plural, glasses, then decided not to think about it. Jon returned to the living room and sat near Mary on the couch. Across from them, relaxed into an armchair beneath a tall reading light, Val skimmed through the manuscript.

The manuscript was both technical and historical, part lab journal and part apology, as if he wanted his work to be clearly understood. He outlined experiments as if they were recipes. Val paused to let that settle, as she realized—he had not been the first to experiment on humans.

Lab journal entries included names and addresses of patients, medical histories, and notes about genetic screening. He had recorded detailed information about all his experimental offspring: gestation periods, weights, hair color, and measurements of limbs, fingers, and toes. He had kept meticulous notes on each baby for three months. Then nothing. If he had seen any of the children later, he hadn't recorded it here.

The manuscript indicated that the procedures for producing polyploids had been perfected in North Korea in the mid-1990s. And he had been there, his first experiments resulting in stillborns.

Then something must have happened. There was no further reference to experiments in North Korea, or at least to Dr. Solven's part in them. His notes indicated he was working in Russia in the summer of 1996, again producing transgenic polyploids. The experiments apparently continued there until December 1997 when he wrote, "These special infants were born healthy."

Dr. Solven explained that producing human polyploids had been an offshoot of discoveries by North Korean scientists working with mice. They had found that exposing zygotes to low doses of the herbicide tridysofon *in vitro* resulted in embryonic cells with double the normal number of chromosomes. These polyploid embryos were implanted in mice uteruses where they developed normally. However, the length of pregnancies was a third of the normal time expected in mice. The new polyploid mice were able to mate and bear a second generation of polyploids. The extremely rapid development and enormous size of the polyploid mice fascinated the North Korean government, which saw the potential for an army of supermen.

The procedures for genetically engineering polyploid humans for parthenogenesis, regeneration, and production of L-asborbic acid, better known as vitamin C, were developed in Russia. Creation of North Korean polyploids predated development of the transgenic delivery system. Dozens of North Koreans, Chinese, and Russian scientists worked feverishly to perfect the polyploids as transgenic warriors. Regeneration allowed wound healing without medical expense, and female warriors could clone efficiently by parthenogenesis. Warriors able to make L-ascorbic acid possibly had an extra measure of health.

Dr. Solven included excerpts from a lecture where he agreed with the Nobel prize-winning biochemist Linus Pauling that L-ascorbic acid could prevent cancer and other common illnesses and infections.

They obtained the gene for biosynthesis of the GULO enzyme needed for making vitamin C from the slow loris (Nycticebus coucang; Lorisidae), a prosimian with large eyes and long tail. The slow loris, along with a vast majority of animals, have genes for synthesizing the four enzymes required to convert glucose to L-ascorbic acid.

In primitive primates of the Strepsirrhini clade, or prosimians, which includes lorises and lemurs, the four steps needed for synthesis of L-ascorbic acid are functional. However, in the primate Haplorrhini clade, or simians, which includes humans, monkeys, and apes, the gene for producing the enzyme L-gulonolactone oxidase, abbreviated GULO, needed for the fourth step, mutated in the common ancestor of the group, blocking their ability to produce L-ascorbic acid.

In 1996, researchers found a strain of mice, the MRL, who were capable of regeneration. These mice could heal holes that had been punched in their ears as identification markers. Scientists at the Wistar Institute discovered that their p21 gene was inhibited.

We used this information to create a mechanism for incorporating small interfering RNAs (siRNAs) to specifically inhibit p21, a cell cycle regulator. The p21 gene is tightly regulated by p53, a tumor suppressor gene. In normal cells, p21 acts to eliminate cells with damaged DNA before they divide out of control and produce cancerous tissue.

Val paused to sip her wine without looking up. She was fascinated.

At first, scientists at Wistar were concerned that mice with non-functioning p21 would show increases in cancer rates. However, they found that although production of cells with damaged DNA occurred at the usual rate, an increase in apoptosis, or programmed cell death, destroyed such cells in the absence of a functioning p21 gene.

A package of desired genes and secret mechanisms were engineered into the lentivirus, a virus capable of invading most any cell membrane. The packaging included the gene for making the GULO enzyme missing in humans, the gene for delivering siRNA to knock out the regeneration inhibiting p21 gene, and a specific gene allowing parthenogenesis.

Parthenogenesis proved to be the most difficult, and the genetics of a nematode helped us work out those steps. We wanted polyploid females to be able to reproduce by cloning and normal sexuality, which necessitated that under certain circumstances, cloning would not occur. For cloning to take place, meiosis in mother cells in the ovary must be inhibited, and for sexual reproduction, meiosis must occur normally.

After in vitro fertilization, the zygotes were bathed for twenty-four hours in media containing genetically engineered lentiviruses and the herbicide, tridysofon.

The herbicide induced tetraploidy in the cells of the developing embryo, and individuals resulting from implanting of these modified embryos were born with the ability to produce L-ascorbic acid, perhaps to reproduce by parthenogenesis, and were capable of regeneration. We had no way to prove that females would be parthenogenetic until they were old enough.

She took a deep breath, and said, "Herbicides. Yes, they change us, and we don't know how."

"What do you mean?" Mary asked.

"I'll explain later." Val sighed, which Mary now echoed, feeling an even stronger warmth for her. Was this also chemistry?

Val was also wondering about chemistry, of reactions beyond our conscious understanding happening all around us. And who wouldn't like to have genes for regeneration?

She had been unaware of the p21 gene in mice and was amazed that inhibiting a single gene could have such profound effects. Mammals were the only organisms incapable of regeneration, or so she had always assumed. Genes for parthenogenesis would override birth control, and that disturbed her. Diploid humans were already over-populating the earth. The political intrigue behind the discoveries made her feel suddenly very uneasy about the manuscript. What if this information fell into the wrong hands? She took a yellow pad from her briefcase and began taking notes.

According to Dr. Solven, 550 polyploids had been created worldwide. And 255 were in Russia and North Korea. The first polyploids had been born in 1995 in North Korea, then in Russia in 1996. The first born in the U.S. had been in 2000 in upstate New York. Dr. Solven had relocated every two years, to Los Angeles, Vermilion, and finally to Houston where he died. He'd practiced in Houston six years. Why had he stayed so long?

Val looked up and rubbed her eyes, realizing she was exhausted. Mary and Jon were no longer sitting on the couch. She had become absorbed in her reading and only vaguely recalled their going to the kitchen together. "Mary, Jon? Where are you?"

She walked down a semi-lit hallway, and found an open doorway that led to an empty bedroom with a bedside light on. Across the hallway, a bathroom. She went on down the hallway and found a second bedroom where Mary and Jon were curled up together on a mattress on the floor. The mattress had been extended with a makeshift combination of pillows and blankets. The sight of their intimacy startled her. She heard her mother's voice telling her she must separate them immediately. But they were asleep, exhausted as she was. She'd bring it up in the morning. Or maybe she wouldn't.

XXXX

Early the next morning, Val awakened to laughter coming from outside. She pulled on a robe she was glad she'd packed, went into the living room, and out through the French doors. Wearing shorts and T-shirts, Mary and Jon were playing like children in the pool. Their innocence made her smile.

Mary saw Val and called her to join them. But she only waved back and followed the aroma of coffee into the kitchen. Sonia, humming, wordlessly poured Val a cup of coffee.

She took her coffee into the living room and, seeing the remote on the side table, turned on the TV. Two handsome young reporters on CNN were describing Michael's arrest. His familiar and troubled face filled one fourth of the screen.

"The gigantic Michael Pitre was subdued by five policemen this morning at a Burger King on Travis Street in downtown Houston." The screen showed a brief clip of police dragging a nearly unconscious Michael to a police car and shoving him head first onto the back seat.

An attractive brunette reporter, standing outside the Burger King, described the arrest. "The man is nearly eight feet tall. As you can see, he doesn't even fit well into the back seat of a normal car. This is an exclusive! You're hearing it here first. He claims to be a polyploid, whatever that is. Before the taser hit him, he yelled that Dr. Solven deserved to die for creating freaks like him. People cleared out of the Burger King as soon as the police began struggling with the giant man. No injuries have been reported."

Mary and Jon, wrapped in towels, came into the living room and stood beside Val.

"Dr. Maximilian Solven was murdered three days ago. Mary Solven, the victim's daughter, Jon Landry, her boyfriend, and Bob Nelson, a driver who worked for the doctor, found Dr. Solven dead in his office at the Solven Fertility Clinic in the 1300 block of St. Mark's Parkway in Houston. According to a statement by Detective Rodriguez, Mary told police they discovered Michael

Pitre in the office with the body. Michael Pitre apparently admitted to them that he killed Dr. Solven."

"What should we do?" Mary asked.

"I don't know," Val said. "But we should all get dressed. We might have company before long."

She could easily imagine that National TV coverage of Michael's arrest would create an outcry against polyploids. The word alone was probably already creating a panic. And what about the other polyploids? Were they still alive? Were they like Mary and Jon? Or were they like Michael?

They had barely started breakfast when Mary's phone rang.

"Yes, this is Mary Solven." ... "Yes, we can come to the police station this morning."

"Detective Rodriguez wants us to identify Michael. Since Bob was a witness, they want to see him too."

And that probably wouldn't be the end of it, Val realized, as they waited for Bob to pick them up. Neither Mary nor Jon was going to Vermilion anytime soon. Once they identified Michael, they'd become key witnesses. If they were lucky, they wouldn't be arrested as giant accomplices.

"What about the house and the clinic, Mary? You could stay here until the police sort out this thing with Michael."

"But Louisiana is my home." Mary felt she needed to be near Val, who reached across the breakfast table for Mary's hand and squeezed it.

"We'll return to Vermilion as soon as we can. But first we must make sure Dr. Solven's manuscript doesn't get into the wrong hands."

"How can we do that?"

"I'm not sure. But for now, if you don't object, Mary, I'm going to keep it in my briefcase. If we leave it here, they'll find it if they search the house. I'm surprised the police haven't already. And we need to know more about what's going on at the clinic, like whose taking care of the lentiviruses and embryos stored there."

"I know one of the doctors, Tom Bradford," Jon said. "I think he'll talk to us. And something else, Dr. Solven's manuscript indicates that his Russian sources for lentiviruses had been secretive about what they engineered into the viruses. The news of Michael's capture and the death of Dr. Solven is bound to have reached Russia by now."

"Yes," Val caught his drift. "They'll know that others could reverse engineer from samples of the viruses. We've got to find out where the viruses and embryos are, before they get in the wrong hands."

"Hello, Dr. Bradford? This is Mary Solven." … "Yes, thanks. I'm fine." … "We're here in Houston, at Dr. Solven's house." … "Yes. I'm hoping you can give us some information." … "My guardian, a biologist, is here with me now. My father gave me his manuscript."

Mary handed the phone to Val, and after a lengthy conversation, she had some of the information she wanted. She was also convinced that Dr. Bradford was an ally and well-aware of the possible consequences of Dr. Solven's death. He assured her that the lentiviruses and embryos were stored in liquid nitrogen in a locked, ventilated cabinet in a laboratory. It was a safe place but hardly bullet-proof.

As Val put down the phone, Mary said, "We have to close the clinic."

XXYY

Bob drove them to the Harris County Facility where Detective Rodriguez had said to meet him. The luxurious River Oaks neighborhood and Houston's jail were in close proximity. The rich and the poor. The parking lot was overflowing with TV cameramen and reporters.

They weren't out of Bob's SUV before reporters shoved microphones at them. Others took pictures; the flashes were blinding. The networks, newspapers, and internet would be flooded with images of giants.

"Did you come to the jail to identify the giant who killed Dr. Solven?"

"Did you witness the killing?"

"How did he do it?"

"How tall are you?"

"What's your name?"

"How old are you?"

"Are you two what they call polyploids?"

Bob guided them across the parking lot and into the facility. Recognizing Mary and Jon, a security guard stopped the reporters at the door. He ushered them into a noisy waiting room, that wasn't a separate room at all, but an extension of a larger room of desks and people who were mostly hurrying from one place to another.

A woman walked toward them. "The detective will be with you soon. Just have a seat there." She pointed to several chairs, and Val noticed the Pitres sitting in a far corner. She left Mary and Jon to talk to them.

"Hello. Remember me? I'm Val Smythe. We met at the meeting at the university. I'm so sorry about Michael. Is there anything I can do?"

Mrs. Pitre spoke softly in her Cajun accent. Simply dressed in a pale green housedress, she sat with her hands folded in her lap as if she were resigned to what might happen. "Yes, I remember you, and the meeting. Everything has gone wrong since."

"It's that doctor's fault," her husband interrupted. "And Michael claims Solven was dead when he arrived at the clinic. He only wanted to talk to him. Now look what's happened."

Val had no time to argue. She saw someone talking to Mary, Jon, and Bob, and hurried toward them.

Detective Rodriquez was saying, "I need you to identify the man in custody as the one you saw in Dr. Solven's office the day he was murdered. You don't have to talk to him."

Val introduced herself, and Rodriguez reluctantly accepted her outstretched hand by the fingertips. "How's Michael?" she asked. "You know he's mentally ill and needs medication. Has he seen a psychiatrist? Your jail has a reputation for depriving prisoners of medical treatment." Going on the offense, without giving her target a chance to respond was an old habit of hers, and she guessed that Houston jails were no better than most.

"Lady, I don't care what you think about HPD jails. Sit down, or I'll have you arrested for interfering with an investigation." He turned to Mary. "Follow me, Miss Solven. I'll be back for you, Mr. Landry, and then you, Mr. Nelson."

Mary followed, towering over the detective. They disappeared through a doorway.

Ten minutes later, Mary and Rodriguez returned, and Jon reached for her hand.

"Come with me," Rodriguez said brusquely to Jon, who remained calm and poised.

Val said, "Are you OK, Mary? You look like you've seen a ghost."

"I'm fine, but Michael isn't. He's been handcuffed and shackled at the ankles. He shuffled, not walked, into the room, and when he saw me, he pleaded for me to help him get out."

Rodriguez returned with Jon, then said to Bob, "I think we can skip your identification. It's clear we have the bad giant." He smirked. "Your old friend, Michael, if he is that, will appear before a judge in a few days. And we'll need you three again as witnesses. You're free for now, but don't think I'm through with you. I still think you're involved in this more than you're admitting."

"Wait," Mary said. "I have a question. How did Michael get those bruises on his face?"

"Are you kidding? Nobody in this jail is strong enough to beat him up. Besides, we had to put him in isolation. He must have beaten himself up. If you have more questions, ask them in court."

As Rodriguez walked off, Jon said, "Man, would I like to be alone with him for ten minutes. But it wouldn't be a fair fight with that pipsqueak. Why does he try to humiliate us?"

Val touched his arm. "Let's ask the guard if there's another, quieter, way out."

CHAPTER 7

As they approached Dr. Solven's house, reporters ran toward their SUV. "Get out of the car so we can see you giants. What's it like being polyploid? What makes you so different?"

Mary and Jon scrunched down, trying to make themselves look smaller.

Bob managed to maneuver the SUV through the crowd without running down anyone and drove as close as he could to the garage door before pushing the remote. Still, some reporters slipped into the garage. Bob closed the door quickly, trapping them inside.

A short woman wearing a baseball cap with "WCET Channel 23" printed across the brim confronted Bob as he got out of the car. She was among five others bold enough to enter the garage. "We want to ask them some questions," she said, as others pushed camera lenses against the tinted car windows.

It occurred to Val that maybe that wasn't such a bad idea. If Mary and Jon answered their questions, maybe that would help appease the crowd outside. Mary and Jon stepped out of the SUV into the garage shadows, and several of the reporters gasped.

"You're Jon Landry, right?" asked the woman in the cap. "How tall are you?" She pushed a microphone up to Jon's face, and a TV cameraman stepped close, looking up at Jon. From that angle, Val thought, Jon will look like something from the Pleistocene.

"I'm seven feet and still growing," Jon said, as if he were talking to a friend.

Another gasp from a reporter. "What do you mean *still* growing?"

Val, worried Jon might reveal his true age, interrupted, "I'm sorry, but it was a mistake to talk with you now. We're preparing for a press conference."

"Who are you?" someone asked.

"I'm a biologist, Dr. Val Smythe. And a friend of the family."

"Biologist? Are you responsible for this freak show? Are there other giants like them out there?"

Val turned her back to the reporter, knowing any answer she gave would lead to more questioning. "It's been a long morning. We're going inside now, and I think you should leave." Val pointed to the side garage door. "Bob and Jon, can you help them out? Jon and Mary's size was enough; the reporters reluctantly backed toward the door, and Bob locked it behind them.

Looks like the end of anonymity for polyploids. And for me too, Val thought, considering the brief introduction she had just given the press.

Before they'd gotten far into the house, Val's phone rang. It was Walt saying that Val was on the news. "That didn't take long," she said.

He summarized. The university president was being interviewed. The department was debating whether they should say they knew Val was in Houston or deny knowledge of her experiment. *Her experiment?* Walt was almost certain the university would stay neutral or even position themselves for taking credit if it turned out to be beneficial for them. Val was overwhelmed with how out of control things were becoming.

"And Val," Walt added, "everyone wants to talk with you—President Dalhousie and Dean Thibodeaux."

"Walt, there's something you need to know. Dr. Solven, gave Mary his manuscript. I've read it, and he not only describes his experiments but also lists the locations of the other polyploids he created. I'm bringing the manuscript with me, to protect it. I'm flying back to Vermilion tonight if I can get a flight, but Mary and Jon can't leave Houston. Michael's hearing is in two or three days."

Then she called David. "The police will know someone forged Michael's driver's license."

While Val had been talking, Mary, Jon, and Bob had been watching themselves on cable news.

Val said, "I hope this ends soon."

"It's not going to end," Mary said. "We're circus freaks. I can see how we look to them."

Val hugged Mary wordlessly, then said, "I have to be in Vermilion tomorrow. But before I go, we need a plan. Polyploids elsewhere will see this news and realize there are others like them. Imagine how confused they might become. I think we should contact them."

"Yes," Jon said.

"We need to get everyone we can to a meeting."

XXXX

Mary and Jon were trapped in the house with the shades down, unable to walk outside for fear of being swarmed by the reporters. The latest cable news episode, billed as the *Killer Giant Story*, focused on Val's leaving the house for the airport.

The anchorman reported dramatically, "Dr. Val Smythe is a biology professor at Vermilion State University. She lives with her husband, an ex-priest. One of the giants, Mary Solven, lived next door to Dr. Smythe and her husband, and she moved in with them when her mother died. Isn't that right, Mr. Pitre?" The camera moved to Mr. Pitre who nodded.

"I'm standing here now with one giant's mother and father at their home in Vermilion, Louisiana." A camera panned the front yard, showing crowds of angry people filling the yard and street. The Pitre's white clapboard house seemed small and lost in all the attention.

"Is there anything you want us to know about your son?" the anchorman asked, holding the microphone to Mr. Pitre.

"Yes. My son Michael is only seven years old and should be tried as a juvenile. He's being held with adult criminals and belongs with juveniles his age. Also, he's mentally ill and needs medication to control his violence. We're afraid he'll hurt himself."

"Seven years old! That's hard to believe. He's well over seven feet tall. So you think he's innocent of the killing?"

"We should know how old he is! We're his parents! I don't know what he did. I wasn't there. He needs help. We tried to get him to a psychiatrist, but he wouldn't go," Mr. Pitre said.

Mary and Jon stared at the screen in disbelief as Mr. Pitre told his story. "He's making things worse for Michael and the rest of us."

Then the anchorman's face filled the TV screen again, as he announced coverage was returning to the studio for breaking news.

"Another polyploid has been seen in the Vermilion mall."

Mary and Jon recognized a girl from the meeting in Vermilion. She was running from the camera.

XXYY

"What are we going to do?" Mary said to Jon. "Even if we could leave here unnoticed, they'd hunt us down. Where could we hide? We're giants." Mary moved closer to Jon on the couch, and he reached for her hand.

They sat close for several minutes. Then Jon gently urged her to her feet and led her to the bedroom, where they undressed each other slowly and made love on the mattress on the floor before falling asleep.

They were awakened by Bob calling to them from the living room. They scrambled into their clothes. "How long has he been back?" Mary asked, noticing the open bedroom door. "Do you think he saw us?"

"Well, it's possible. We left the door open." Jon laughed.

They found Bob watching the news in the living room.

"Hi Bob. Did Val make her flight?" Mary asked, realizing she wasn't embarrassed.

"I assume she will. I dropped her off at the departure gate. We lost the paparazzi, so she had some peace. She said she'd call you. Are you kids hungry? I stopped at Sonic on the way back to get chili dogs."

"You bet we are!" Jon exclaimed, pushing Mary's shoulder playfully.

Bob put the warm bags splotched with grease and tomato sauce on plates on the dining room table. As Mary wiped chili from her mouth after her fourth chili dog, Val called to say that her flight was leaving in an hour. Mary said they had emailed a short note to all the polyploids they'd located from Dr. Solven's manuscript. They'd signed Val's name.

Dear friends,

By now you have seen news reports about polyploids and know what your children are. Dr. Solven, for his own reasons, did not tell you that he implanted polyploid embryos in his in vitro fertilizations.

I'm writing this letter to suggest that you contact other parents and that we meet. I've included addresses of polyploids in your area that Dr. Solven had in his notes. The sooner we meet, the better things will be for all of you.

Sincerely,

Dr. Valerie Smythe

"I have an idea," Bob said. "Why don't you set up a blog? I'm sure you can learn how, and it's how a lot of people get information now. It might be another way to reach other people like you, and it would give you a forum to express your own views and show that you, Jon, and the others aren't like Michael."

"I hope the others aren't like Michael," Mary said. "I know a little something about blogs, and Jon, if you help, I'm sure we can set it up. What should we call it?"

Jon pulled up a chair beside Mary at the computer. "I like *New Humans* as the group name. After all, that's what we are," he said. "We're a new race and maybe a new subspecies. Hey, why not give ourselves an unofficial scientific name? I'm sure the scientists who officially name species will ignore whatever we call ourselves. But it could be fun. I've never named anything before."

"Then what about subspecies *biggamania* or *biggapersonia*?" Mary suggested.

"Catchy," Jon said, "and it indicates our size. What about *megabodia* or *gigabodia*?"

"No," Mary responded, "*bodia* isn't Latin. Should it be *megacorpus*?"

"No, that sounds like big corpse," Jon said. "How about *morpha* for form as in *gigamorpha*, meaning big form."

"That makes us sound fat. Speak for yourself, but I'm not fat,"

Mary said. "*Novomorph* for new body describes us."

"Our bodies aren't new, just a variation. Unless you have an extra limb I haven't seen." He chuckled.

"OK. How about a name that refers to our multiple chromosome number? That's what really makes us different from *Homo sapiens* subspecies *sapiens*. Chromosome means colored body, so we can use the *soma*, or body, part of the word and give it a Latin twist," Mary said, becoming serious again.

"*Poly*, meaning many, combined with *soma* is *polysoma*," Jon said.

"Let's give it a reasonable ending like *sapiens*. That makes it *polysomiens*," Mary said.

"That's it, Mary. *Homo sapiens* subspecies *polysomiens*."

"First a name, then a statement of purpose," Jon said, and both he and Mary began offering ideas. Bob, who was beginning to think his role had expanded from driver to protector of giants, sat by a window, watching the activity on the lawn. He listened while Mary and Jon brainstormed. It was clear to him that although they were bigger and smarter, they weren't threatening, at least not to him.

Not much later, Jon and Mary had a draft.

Here—we hope to provide an online community for polyploids and their families, where we can share information and resolve problems. In the last few weeks, we have learned a great deal about ourselves. We grew up without knowing that we were genetically different. Through the efforts of Dr. Val Smythe and Dr. Walter Klein, we now know that we're polyploids. We shared this information at a meeting in Vermilion that many of you attended.

"OK. That's the purpose. What do you think?"

"Looks good to me," Jon said.

"What should our first post say?" Mary asked.

"Let's say we're in love." Jon laughed, leaning his head on her shoulder. She kissed his forehead, and they worked.

After the meeting in Vermilion, Louisiana, we learned that

Dr. Solven created polyploids in his fertility clinics. Besides our great height, we also share other features (we think): growing to adulthood by age five or six, physically and mentally, and having the capacity for regeneration. We make vitamin C, and we are parthenogenetic, which means our parthenogenetic genes allow spontaneous pregnancies without sexual intercourse.

Dr. Solven moved his fertility clinic from state to state. His first clinic in the United States was in New York, and from there, he moved to Los Angeles, Vermilion, and Houston. Before arriving in this country, Dr. Solven worked in North Korea and in his native Russia, where he and dozens of scientists honed the techniques for making polyploids and inserting genes.

Please feel free to comment.

XXXX

Mary was awakened in the still darkness to the sounds of Sonia making breakfast in the kitchen. Sonia was singing softly, heavenly, as if the world outside had no interest in her, as if some land far away was here in this darkness comforting everyone. How had she gotten by the reporters? Mary slipped out of bed and went to the window, pulling the curtain aside. The yard and street were clear. What had happened? She turned to tell Jon, but saw he was still sleeping soundly, and she resisted the urge to wake him. Instead she put on a robe and went to the study.

She checked the responses to their new blog and was surprised to find that seventy-five people had joined the group. Many had posted messages. Some thanked her for setting up the group. Some described themselves. One polyploid girl, Martha, wrote that she was pregnant but vehemently insisted she was a virgin. Martha's mother posted a message corroborating her story. Mary recognized Martha as the girl who had been running from reporters in the Vermilion mall last night.

The genes he put into our DNA are rearing their ugly head, Mary thought. For him, making polyploids parthenogenetic was a major triumph. But what if they all started having babies uncontrollably? He had written in the manuscript that he was uncertain whether the genes would function. Now you have an answer... Father.

Mary wondered when parthenogenesis would kick in for her. She thought bitterly that perhaps inception was a better word than conception, since the prefix *con* meant with. In parthenogenesis there was no with anybody else.

Mary turned on the TV to see if the polyploids were still being covered by the news media. Nothing. The media had moved on to a new disaster brewing in the Atlantic. Another oil rig very near Boston was on red alert. Mary felt alarm and sadness for those threatened people. But she sighed relief that for the moment the polyploids were out of the limelight.

By afternoon, three more girls wrote that they were also pregnant virgins. That led to numerous questions about the implications of parthenogenesis. Why had he inserted such genes? Will all polyploid women become pregnant? What triggers parthenogenesis? Stress? What would happen to them?

Mary posted: "I think my father wanted to insure the future of polyploids. I don't think he knew what would actually work. So he covered his bets with parthenogenesis, even though such offspring would be female clones of their mothers. But he couldn't know whether we could reproduce sexually. And I doubt he knew we would start reproducing at six years old! OK. If you're so smart, figure it out."

Mary knew the implication of what she'd just written. If we can (and did!) reproduce every six years, the world would be overrun with giants in a very short time. If the "normal" diploid humans realized that, the polyploids would be in even more trouble. But we don't even know if any of the children will survive!

A few minutes later, as if reading Mary's mind, Val sent a message to the group: "As for the triggering of parthenogenesis, stress could be a factor. Stress on polyploids has increased since Michael's arrest for the murder of Dr. Solven. For now, you're like rock stars of the media, but when they find out how superior you are mentally, they'll view you as a dangerous threat. Since 'normal' humans outnumber you, they could quarantine you. Governments might even say it's for your own protection."

As if reading Val's mind, another polyploid, Paul Martin, posted: "We need to be independent of the normal human world. I suggest we form a community in an isolated place. We'll need to provide our own utilities and infrastructure: shelter, food, water, and electricity. We can develop methods of raising food on small amounts of land. With our intelligence, we can do this."

Val, Jon, Mary, and anyone else who was interested read.

"My father is a building contractor. I learned to build and to do electrical and plumbing work. An engineer at NanoSol and I invented an inexpensive house coating that captures solar energy and transfers it to a battery bank. My parent's home is totally off the grid, and we can do the same in our village."

By day's end, many more polyploids had posted messages, offering to help contribute to their new community.

"Jon, I think we have the talent," Mary said. "And we should be able to get money from selling the clinic's buildings. After all, I am my father's heir. But we need land, preferably as isolated as possible."

Jon took Mary's seat at the computer, while she thumbed through a statistics book she discovered in Dr. Solven's library. "Let's do it, Mary. What about buying land around Arath where Val's dad lives? It's isolated and has rice and crawfish farms. It's near the coast where we could fish for seafood. Ask Val what she thinks about building there. Her father probably knows some farms for sale. I even have a name for the town. It's *Polysomia*, after our subspecies name."

Mary's phone rang. She listened quietly as Val told her that David had been arrested for forgery.

CHAPTER 8

During breakfast, Val read Father Landry's column in the Monday *Daily News* that David had saved for her. Landry, one of the priests at St. Joseph's Roman Catholic Church in Vermilion, was popular among Catholics in the area, and he apparently voiced the sentiments of many non-Catholics as well. In every sermon since Michael's hearing, Landry had warned his parishioners about polyploids. He said they posed dangers to the lives of the faithful, and he cited news items about Mary and Jon. His column alarmed her, and she stopped reading. She had enough to worry about besides the religious conservatives. And despite her concern for David, she knew she had to keep her appointment with the university president.

A large antique mahogany desk dominated President Henri Dalhousie's office. Pictures of smiling jockeys standing beside horses adorned with winning ribbons decorated his walls. Ray Thibodeaux, Dean of the College of Science, was sitting beside the president.

"Val," Dalhousie said, "we know about your recent activities, and we're very interested in the polyploids. I'll get to the reasons in a moment. Considering your natural curiosity about them, you must know more than you've revealed in the media coverage."

Val's dark skin concealed the heat rising in her face. "I realize that I should have informed the administration about my travels. I've been able to meet all my classes, but no doubt, I've caused embarrassment to the university. I didn't expect my visit to Houston to be newsworthy, or I'd have warned you. I apologize."

Val hadn't realized that she had stood until the president motioned her to return to her chair. "On the contrary, we see this as a wonderful opportunity for the university." The president looked to the dean for affirmation and to take the lead.

"Val," Thibodeaux began, "I've read your papers on plant polyploids that Jerry was kind enough to copy. Mathematics is my expertise, but I gleaned the information I needed. We want you to lead a new Department of Polyploid Studies. We can see interactions with the humanities, for example, the Departments of Sociology and Psychology. What do you think?"

"I'm completely taken aback. I'll have to think about this. It's true that polyploidy is my expertise, but in plants, not humans."

"It seems to me that there are no professed experts on polyploid humans except Dr. Solven, who's dead," Thibodeaux said. "I think you're perfect for the job; the polyploids are in your backyard, so to speak."

Dalhousie jumped back in confidently. "The university would benefit greatly from being in the forefront of such studies."

"My only concern is objectivity," Thibodeaux said. "Val is too personally involved with Mary Solven to be objective."

"I don't think her objectivity is an issue. We have proof that Mary is a polyploid, don't we, Val?" Dalhousie asked.

She hesitated, then said, "Yes, Walt Klein has confirmed it."

"If I promise to substantially increase your current salary, would you decide right here and now? You'll have no teaching duties and can begin a faculty search immediately. There will be other enticements for them to join. Now have I enticed you?"

Stunned and suspicious, Val asked, "How many people do you have in mind? That will require substantial funding."

"You tell me how many and who you want. I'll find the funding. Eventually of course, I'll expect you to bring in grant support, but the university will be happy to help you get started. Val, this could be big. Put us on the map! What do you say?"

"Well, I like the idea, Henri. But before I give a final answer, there's a private matter I need to discuss with you." David's arrest was the last thing she wanted to bring up, but she knew Henri knew people.

"My husband has been arrested, and his arrest involves the polyploids. He forged identification for Michael Pitre, Dr. Solven's killer. Before he was Dr. Solven's killer, I mean, and before we really knew what was going on with the polyploids. David was just trying to help him out. He's not really a forger, just a photographer. Then Michael decided to tell the police about the forgery, hoping he'd be tried as a juvenile."

Dalhousie thought a minute, then said, "I think this is a perfect example of the need for a Department of Polyploid Studies, to clear up some of this confusion about who they are. Unfortunately, forgery is federal, so we can't handle that here in Louisiana. I'll need to call an old buddy of mine in D.C. But don't you worry, I'll handle this. Your husband will be home before you are. You get to work on our new department."

XXYY

The doorbell rang, and Mary opened the door to a man wearing a badge. "I'm from the sheriff's office, here to serve Mary Solven and Jon Landry with subpoenas. Are you Mary Solven?"

She nodded.

"Then you've been served." He handed her the papers.

Mary called Val, who said she'd return to Houston as soon as she could. She'd tell Henri she was recruiting, getting important information, but she didn't mention the new department to Mary.

XXXX

On Thursday morning, the reporters were back, and they surrounded the SUV as Bob backed out of the garage. Although he had questioned his purchase of an SUV (who needed four-wheel drive in Houston?), he was glad now for its high ride. He turned sharply and sped ahead of several vans that now followed them.

"I feel sick," Mary said. "I think I have to throw up."

"Please stop, Bob," Jon said.

Jon jumped from the backseat to help her out. Then he put his hand on her back as she leaned over to vomit beside the highway. Vans stopped, and photographers preserved the vivid details.

Later, Mary would watch the coverage: "The driver had to pull over for Mary Solven to vomit. Fear must have caused the famous polyploid to be sick on her way to the preliminary hearing of Michael Pitre, the giant who murdered her father. Her enormous boyfriend, with whom she's been living in her father's house, was beside her."

Back in the SUV, Mary calculated to herself. We had sex for the first time only three weeks ago. But this can't mean... Could polyploid pregnancies be that short?

At the courthouse, a noisy crowd swarmed them as they hurried across the parking lot where armed officers met and led them inside.

Michael was also being escorted into the courtroom. The shirtsleeves and pants of his orange jail scrubs were too short for his long limbs. He looked like something out of a fairy tale, an unhappy one. His scruffy beard looked as if he hadn't shaved in days. He shuffled to his seat, his dark eyes finding a painted mural, dulled from time, behind the judge's dais. A man holding a moneybag was bent to the ground. Two men held clubs above him.

Michael's hearing would decide whether sufficient evidence existed to try him for Dr. Solven's murder. Michael pleaded not guilty.

Detective Rodriguez came to the witness stand and described the murder scene. "Yes," he said, "Michael confessed to killing Dr. Solven at the time of his arrest."

"He's lying! I didn't confess! You, you... I never told you anything!" Michael yelled, rattling his handcuffs. His wild hair, swung from side to side, adding to his appearance of madness. He lunged toward the judge's bench. Two policemen moved immediately to restrain him.

"Mr. Pitre, please go back to your seat and keep quiet," the judge said, nervously gripping his gavel.

"I will not let him lie about me! And take off these chains." Michael shook his cuffs. "They tortured me!"

"Mr. Pitre, sit down and keep quiet, or I'll have you removed from my court!"

Michael turned to audience, "Mary, Jon. You can help me. You know he deserved to die."

"Remove him from my court!"

Several additional policemen surrounded Michael, and led him from the courtroom. The judge pounded his gavel several times.

"Is there any other evidence of Mr. Pitre's guilt, Detective?"

"Yes. DNA from skin found under the fingernails of Dr. Solven matched Michael Pitre's DNA. One of the witnesses described seeing deep scratches on the defendant's neck. However, when Mr. Pitre was captured three days later, we found no scratches."

"How do you explain that?" Michael's attorney cross-examined. "The skin must have come from somewhere. Were the witnesses mistaken about the scratches, or were there scratches elsewhere on Mr. Pitre?"

"There were no other scratches on Mr. Pitre," Rodriguez said.

Suddenly, Michael reappeared in the doorway and almost made his way to the witness stand before numerous policemen tackled him and held him to the floor. Within seconds, Michael stopped struggling.

"It's clear to the court that Michael Pitre is incapable of standing trial," the judge said. "I order him to be taken to Mercy Hospital for psychiatric examination. This hearing is adjourned."

XXYY

Jon and Mary estimated that their baby was due in two and a half months. Since they no longer had to stay in Houston, they returned to Vermilion and moved into Mary's condo.

To bless their relationship, Val, David, and Jon's family arranged a non-legally binding wedding ceremony in the condo courtyard. To avoid attracting further attention, they didn't invite their new polyploid friends or post information about the wedding on the blog. Still, Val knew they were being watched. But she wouldn't let that spoil the moment. It was Mary and Jon's day.

Belle had lengthened Val's wedding dress, and Mary looked lovely in the ivory strapless gown. Belle had also altered a suit for Jon, and the young couple walked elegantly through the courtyard garden. Moss hung from the live oaks. Azaleas were in full purple bloom, and where green hedges of Camellias came together, a woman with auburn hair, dressed in a red sequined gown, sang. She was accompanied by a pianist who played an electronic keyboard and harmonized enchantingly.

David, the officiant of the ceremony, began, "Welcome to this celebration of the relationship between Mary Solven and Jon Landry. The narrowness of the law forbids a legal marriage of this couple, but it cannot forbid a union of their hearts." He paused, then said, "Mary and Jon would like to say something to each other."

Mary went first. "Jon, father of my child, although our future is uncertain, my feelings for you are everlasting. In my heart, you are my husband. I vow to be your ally and to nurture, love, and care for you for as long as I live."

Then Jon said, "Mary, regardless of how anyone else views this wedding, I vow to be your husband. You will be the only woman in my life. I will love and cherish you, and I am proud that we are the first polyploid parents to bear a child."

Jon wanted this to be true, but he knew sexual unions could have resulted in children in North Korea and Russia, and he also knew that could be another problem for all of them.

XXXX

At breakfast the next morning, David handed Val more bad news, a newspaper article he had been reading with his coffee.

"This guy sounds like he's writing a sermon, not objective news."

Val read aloud, "What do your children think when they see such mocking of wedding vows on TV? I'll tell you; they think the laws of God don't matter anymore. They will think we can flaunt His laws at will and without consequence. Where are our government officials? Every good Christian needs to let them know we want the antics of polyploids stopped before it's too late for us and our children." Val slammed the paper down. "Father Landry is going to be trouble."

As she was opening the door to her office at the university, one of the secretaries caught up to her and spoke in a hushed tone.

"Dr. Smythe, Senator Terrill's secretary called this morning and made an appointment with you. The senator is a friend of President Dalhousie, and there's also a message from him. He said to call him if you had any questions. Senator Terrill needed to catch a flight and will be here this morning."

By ten a.m., Terrill was in her office. He said little more than hello until he had unbuttoned his suit jacket and loosened his red chili pepper tie.

"May I call you Val?"

She nodded.

"I'm afraid I have some very bad news for the polyploids. Because of the publicity surrounding the arrest and trial of Michael Pitre, things are heating up in Congress. Polyploids are now considered a threat to national security, to public safety, to the environment, you name it. And the churches are worked up, as always. Ministers are telling their congregations, and anyone else who will listen, that polyploids are an abomination."

"That's ridiculous!" Val said. "They aren't violent. Michael Pitre has mental problems, like normal people do sometimes." She reconsidered her use of the word normal but didn't correct herself.

Terrill continued. "Here's the bad news. Congress is planning a full-scale investigative hearing on the polyploid issue. And this is going to fall under the jurisdiction of the U.S. Senate Homeland Security Permanent Subcommittee on Investigations. You know what that means. Anything goes if it means national security. Subpoenas for Solven Fertility Clinic records will go out in a few days."

"This smacks of the McCarthy hearings. I thought we were long past witch hunts," Val said.

"It's the same committee, just different people. And no, we never get past witch hunts. We just call them something else."

"When is this happening?" Val asked.

"As soon as they get the paperwork together. Meanwhile, tell the polyploids to keep their heads down. This thing could easily get out of hand. The less normal people know about the polyploids, the better."

"But why are you warning us? Are you on the committee?"

"Yes, I am, and I'll do what I can to keep this thing from getting out of control."

"But why?"

"Let's just say I have my reasons."

XXYY

Val let Mary know the blog site had to come down. Naively, Val had assumed that their blog would just be for polyploids. Now she realized that nothing about the internet, blogs, email, whatever, could be kept private. From what she could gather from Senator Terrill, a lot of people already knew too much about the polyploids, and especially too much about Mary.

But the blog had been useful. Mary had compiled enough information from bloggers to know that polyploid development had indeed occurred earlier in other parts of the United States.

One boy claimed he was the leader of a group of polyploids that had formed after Michael's arrest. They were hiding out, living in remote mountains in upstate New York. Fortunately, their parents were helping them. But it was becoming less likely they could remain hidden. Was there a plan to keep all the polyploids together? He added that most of *them* in New York were between nine and eleven years old. They were exceptionally intelligent, as tall or taller than Mary and Jon, and some were parents! The mothers had conceived, as if on cue, when they were seven years old.

CHAPTER 9

A month passed with no word of the Senate hearing. And Michael's trial seemed on indefinite hold, old news, as he effectively disappeared from the public radar. Surprisingly, no one came forth to contest Dr. Solven's will, and his house and clinic were transferred to a trust in Mary's name. Then when Val was appointed trustee and Mary's age was never mentioned, Val suspected Senator Terrill had arranged everything. Events were happening too quickly and going too smoothly to allow Val to feel comfortable about any of this. Even the financial issues that should have caused problems with her new department were dissolving without issue.

No one came forward to protest Mary's decision to close the clinic. So in keeping with the Department of Health's Code of Practice for Records Management, Dr. Bradford rented a climate controlled storage unit and stored all the clinic's maternity records. They would be kept for twenty-five years after the last birth. He also agreed to destroy the embryos and lentivirus materials Dr. Solven had stored in liquid nitrogen at the clinic. Then the trust sold the clinic to a group of oil magnates.

That night, to celebrate closing the clinic sale, David prepared one of his specialties, Creole shrimp, for Val, Mary, and Jon. After everyone had enjoyed a few mouthfuls of shrimp, he asked, "What will you do with the money, Mary?"

"The trust, you mean." She looked at Val. "We want to buy land to build a sustainable, independent place for polyploids, Jon and I already have a name for the community: Polysomia. Do you have any ideas about where we can buy land?"

"How many other polyploids are interested in living in Polysomia?" Val asked.

"I think most, if not all, the Louisiana polyploids. The others that we've been in close contact with, in New York and Los Angeles, want to form their own communities. Plus, they're there. We're here. I'm not sure it's a good idea to try to get everyone together. We think there might be safety in small numbers."

"Good idea," David said.

"We'd also like to make the community as secluded as possible." Mary paused. "What about a farm around Arath? Grandpa Smythe would know what's for sale, and that's a remote area."

Val noticed that Mary called Hank "Grandpa." He'd said when he first heard about Mary's pregnancy that he was delighted he'd be a great-grandpa. Val wondered where that left her, a professor who had chosen her career over raising a family. That is, until now, when a family seemed to have chosen her.

"Have you thought about how much land you'll need, Mary?"

"Yes, I think we need several hundred acres. We'll need room for buildings, say twenty or twenty-five acres, and the rest we can farm. We should plan to grow our own food and be as self-sustaining as possible."

"OK, let's go to Arath tomorrow. I'll tell Dad and Mom to expect us a day early. It's short notice, but Mom can always find food for a crowd, or we could pick up some seafood dinners in Delcambre." Skipping work on a Saturday would feel like a holiday to Val. And even now, David's escape from a prison sentence was cause for celebration. Everything had happened so quickly; seeing her mom and dad on the farm always helped slow the pace.

Val also noticed Mary moving slowly. Because of her huge belly, even walking through doorways required carefulness. And Jon had grown in the short time since Michael's hearing. When would he stop growing?

XXXX

The growing family once again drove through the flat fields of rice that dominated southwestern Louisiana. Until a couple of decades after the Civil War, a wilderness of nearly 2.5 million acres of low-lying tallgrass prairie stretched over the southwestern quarter of Louisiana. After the building of the railroad from Houston to New Oreleans, the discovery that the rich prairie soil supported rice cultivation attracted farmers from the North and the Midwest. Native prairie land in Louisiana now occupied a meager hundred acres.

Val's dad knew of two rice farms for sale within five miles of Arath. The owners were old family friends. Hank knew they wanted to retire, and their heirs weren't interested in farming.

"Both tracts have made a lot of rice and crawfish over the years. Do you plan to farm, Mary?" Hank asked.

"Yes, we want to grow our food and build houses where other polyploids can live. I don't think we can continue living with regular people. We need a safe place to raise our baby."

"I can teach you to farm. And if you want to sell some of the crops, I can put your rice and crawfish in with mine. That way you'll be anonymous. You could shrimp too. Arath is a half-mile from the coast. Eat some and sell the rest."

"Thanks, Grandpa," Mary said, but she suddenly wasn't looking well.

"Are you OK?" Val asked.

"I don't know. I feel so heavy. I need to lie down."

Jon rushed to her side.

"Help her to our bed," Belle said.

Mary leaned on Jon. They walked slowly down the hall to Hank and Belle's bedroom. Family pictures lined the walls, but they were too focused on getting Mary to the bed to notice anything but her. Belle bent over Mary, checking her pulse, and realizing how hot Mary's skin was, said, "*Chère*, I think your baby is coming."

Val, who stood on the other side of Mary, said, "I don't think we can risk taking her to a hospital."

But before Belle and Val could make a plan, Mary said, "Oh, I think my water just broke. I'm going to ruin your bed, Grandma. I need to get out of this bed and on the floor."

"Oh no, Mary. You're fine on our bed," Belle said.

Ignoring Belle, Mary tried to get up, and Jon was beside her, helping her sit up and onto the floor. She squatted, while Jon steadied her, kneeling behind her to hold her back. Instinctively, Mary took deep breaths and pushed hard.

"Grandma, don't let the baby fall on the floor," Mary said. Her face reddened, and the blood vessels in her neck and forehead began to bulge with the strain. She seemed in a hurry to push the baby out.

Val found the presence of mind to run to the kitchen to warm water to bathe the mother and baby. Only Jon was truly calm. He spoke softly in Mary's ear as she pushed. Belle had only watched the birthing of her sister's and cousin's children, and she hadn't really helped much. Despite the lack of birthing expertise in the room, the baby's head began to crown beneath Mary. Soon a slick, blood-streaked baby boy emerged. Val felt a rush of relief and wondered again at the intensity of her maternal feelings for Mary. Although the entire process had taken only thirty minutes, it felt like hours to Val, and it would likely have been hours for a diploid human being.

To everyone's surprise except Mary's, Jon said, "His name is Peter."

Belle knew enough to tie off the umbilical cord and cut it with her sewing scissors. She washed Peter, wrapped him in a white towel, and handed him to Mary. Peter's thick, red hair matched hers.

"He's such a big baby. If he could walk, I'd think he was a year old," Hank said. "Let's weigh him." At that moment, Peter turned away from his mother, scanned the room, and smiled, as if glad to see the light.

Hank took Peter from Mary and carried him into the bathroom next to the bedroom. Everyone, including Mary, tried to crowd in. He weighed himself with and without Peter. "One ninety-six with him and one seventy-four without. Twenty-two pounds. *Poo yii*, he's a whopper!"

"I'm so hungry, Grandma," Mary said. "Could you fix me one of your big breakfasts?"

"Fried eggs? Grits? Bacon and biscuits?" Belle said. "I'll bring it to you in bed."

"No need, Grandma. I'll come to the table."

By now, no one was surprised at anything Mary did, including her sudden recovery and appetite.

"OK, then. I'll make enough for everybody."

By the time Mary had finished eating, she seemed fully recovered, but Jon urged her to be cautious. She brushed him off.

"Let's look for a farm where we can raise Peter."

Val, more stressed than anyone from the past few hours, could only think now of the implications of the sex of Mary's child. A boy child could only have been conceived sexually, Val thought. A parthenogenetic baby would have been a female clone of Mary. She didn't want to bring that up now, but she wanted to tell Walt as soon as possible. A polyploid human had conceived sexually and borne a seemingly healthy baby. That was news in any biology lab in the universe.

XXYY

Hank inquired about the properties. Mr. Poitier's thousand-acre farm seemed promising.

"Old Poitier wants twenty-five hundred an acre for the land," Hank said. "Then another fifty thousand for a three thousand-square-foot farmhouse, barn, two tractors, and machinery. He wants to sell, and I bet he'll accept a lower offer. It's been on the market several years."

"That's over two and a half million, Mary," Val said. "Almost half the trust money."

"Let's look at it," Mary said.

"Poitier said he'd be around all afternoon," Hank said.

They all wanted to have a look. The family progression of three cars drove the five-mile ride to Poitier's farm. The dirt road leading to his place was deeply rutted and rough.

"We'll have to pave this road someday," Mary said, anticipating ownership of the farm.

The two-story farmhouse built of old cypress in the local Acadian cabin style, had a tin roof and surrounding porch. A tall pole-barn sheltered a combine for harvesting rice, a smaller tractor for ditching crawfish ponds, and an assortment of other farming machinery.

Mr. Poitier, a man about Hank's age, greeted them in overalls, short-sleeved denim shirt, and the ubiquitous white rubber boots worn by crawfish farmers, including Hank. "So dis is your granddaughter, Smythe. *Mais* yeah, she's taller than you. And looks like she picked a tall partner. *Poo yii!* I've seen the news about you all, and I see why you want to get away from that mess. Look at this little one. Boy or girl?"

"This is Peter," Mary answered, teasing a smile from her newborn. "He's a few hours old."

"*Poo yii*! How you do dat, so quick and him grow so big too? Dis granddaughter you got is something else, friend. My wife took forever wit' our little ones, and she ain't got well quick, no."

He hadn't lived in the house since his wife died and apologized for the thick dust covering the scant furniture left inside. "I moved into town when Lorna died, like she always wanted us to," Poitier said. "Shoulda' done it before she died, but I always needed a lil' more money."

Hank patted his friend on the shoulder to console him as best he could. "You never know, old man. Being with you made her happy."

The house needed work, but Mary loved it. "Let's look at the rest of the farm."

Val's motherly instincts resurfaced. "Do you feel up to that, Mary? The ride will be rough. You could sit here in the swing and wait for us."

Jon said, "Yes, stay and rest. Grandpa Hank is the only one who can judge the quality of a rice farm anyway."

"I want to look at every inch of this property," Mary said.

"I'll drive my pick-up," Poitier said. Mary and the baby can sit in the cab with me. You all sit in the back."

Poitier drove around the acres of bright green rice on a perimeter road and stopped the truck halfway around. "I'm asking twenty-five hundred, but considering my old friend Smythe, I'll go to two million for everyt'ing; dat's house, barn, and equipment."

"You call that friendship? Charging my granddaughter and her young family two million dollars!" Hank faked a frown for Poitier's benefit.

"OK, you old cheat! I'm goin' nineteen-fifty an acre for the land and dat's dat!"

"Me, I think, you've been trying to sell this rundown place a long time. Is that about right?"

"I been lookin' for the right neighbor for you, and now I found 'em," Poitier replied, trying to hide a grin.

"Well, I think eighteen hundred is too much," Hank said, frowning but clearly enjoying the bargaining.

"*Mais*, I need to charge you for the gas to drive around this place. You wantin' me to starve in my old age, and you my friend, huh?" Poitier said. "OK, eighteen hundred. And don't come back with no more numbers, *friend*. You got money to pay, I hope. I ain't wantin' to hold no lien. You know you takin' this crop of rice from me, too. But dat's awright, I ain't waitin' on it."

That settled it. Jon barely concealed his excitement, and Mary hugged Poitier.

XXXX

A few weeks later, Val and David arrived to see the farm for the first time since Mary and Jon moved in. Mary rushed from the kitchen doorway to hug Val. "Guess what?" she asked, and without waiting for Val's response, "Bob is coming."

Then Val was truly surprised to see Jon walking from a shed with Peter. Walking!

"I emailed the Texas polyploids and asked who wanted to live here," Mary said. "I think everyone wants to come. They're all coming next weekend to see the farm. Bob's driving the bus!"

"We're having a picnic," Belle said, coming out of the kitchen.

"And a meeting," Jon said. "A lot of families weren't at the meeting in Vermilion."

"What about inviting Walt and his family and the rest of your department, Val?" Mary asked. "Perhaps they should get to know us?"

Val considered a moment, then agreed. "Invite Dr. Bradford, too. He and Walt will have a lot to talk about."

"Of course," Mary said, "I'm glad you remembered him. I couldn't have destroyed the embryos myself. Some were probably our siblings." She realized she hadn't been sure about that decision before, and perhaps she wasn't sure about it now.

"So how are things progressing with the new place?" David reeled in the topic.

"Jon has nearly finished restoring this old farmhouse. Once we told our polyploid friend, Paul, what we were doing, he arrived the next day. He's been so helpful, with remodeling and plumbing the bathrooms and kitchen. Jon has learned a lot from him."

The house had been built to accommodate several large families, typical of Roman Catholic Cajuns.

"The furnishings are sparse, right now," Jon said. "We're building to accommodate our height and weight. Paul and I are making most of the doorways larger, but the fourteen-foot ceilings of these old houses are ready-made for giants. It makes you wonder if giants didn't live here before." He chuckled at his joke.

But Belle said, "Giants did live on the earth. You can read about it in the Bible."

Val was about to launch into her usual argument about how science had demonstrated inaccuracies in the Bible. Then another thought occurred to her; these were giants! And if there were giants right here in front of her, why couldn't there have been giants before? She held her tongue.

"Paul helped me build large walk-in closets in the bedrooms. Families back then stored clothes in armoires," Jon said. "A metal fabricator in Pennsylvania is making aluminum beds for us that bear up to six hundred pounds and hold a custom-made ten-by-twelve-foot mattress and box springs. I sent them the dimensions, and they say they'll manufacture a prototype and ship it to us next week. Mary and I will sleep in a bed instead of a makeshift mattress on the floor."

Outside, Jon pointed to the shimmering rooftop. "We covered the roof with the solar paint Paul invented. It supplies all our electrical needs." He opened the door to a large room. "In here are batteries for storing the energy we need on cloudy days."

"That's a smart husband you have, Mary," Hank said. "We need to put that on our roof, Belle. I bet we could save a ton of money."

"That's not all, Grandpa," Jon said. "Instead of digging wells for water, we built a catchment system on the roof. Rainwater is piped from there to an underground storage cistern, purified, and pumped into the house using solar power. As much as it rains here, we should have enough water if we conserve."

XXYY

Mary and Jon started preparing for the picnic at dawn. Belle and Hank brought drinks in washtubs full of ice, and Val and David arrived mid-morning to help. Jon arranged his new picnic tables in the front yard, and Belle covered them with red-checkered paper cloths. Hank directed guests to park on the grass behind the barn and house, which Jon had freshly mowed for the occasion. The long tables were soon billowing with food.

Val watched as Mary responded warmly to university professors and polyploids alike. Mary's dream of forming a community was occurring before her eyes. Jon pulled Mary up to the wide cypress-planked porch. With Hank's help, they blew bugles to get everyone's attention.

"I'm Mary Solven, and this is my husband, Jon Landry." She put her arm around him. "Welcome to our home, and we hope you'll consider making it your home too."

Val walked behind the house to answer the cell phone vibrating in her pocket. "Yes, Senator Terrill, this is Dr. Smythe" ... "Yes, we're having a picnic on the farm Mary bought near Arath. You're in Vermilion?" ... "Oh, would you like to come?"

Terrill arrived ten minutes later, clearly not in Vermilion, but probably within sight of the farm when he called. He was escorted by three other cars that stopped several hundred yards from the picnic. Terrill's car continued slowly and stopped a short walking distance from the party.

"I always seem to be the bearer of bad news," Terrill said after seating himself on the porch with a big plate of food. "The Senate committee for the polyploid hearing has been selected, and I've managed to get on it. But the others come from among the most conservative members of Congress. I have to tell you that a few senators have been meeting privately to discuss a solution to the polyploid question."

Val was startled. "Why have the hearing now?"

Terrill took a large bite of his shrimp and oyster Po'Boy and said, "Not surprisingly, knowing my opinion, the others have tried to exclude me from their deal-making, but I have spies." He talked with his mouth full of food. "Haven't had one of these in ages. Man, it's good! One thing they agree on is that polyploids need to be isolated from regular people. Their latest idea is to put polyploids on reservations with the American Indians and have them sign a treaty like those folks had to do. Under the treaty agreement, the Department of the Interior would take over jurisdiction of polyploids, as it has over American Indians through the Bureau of Indian Affairs. They've located reservations with enough room in New York, California, Louisiana, and Texas."

"Where in Louisiana?" Val asked.

"The Chitimacha Reservation. It's closest to Vermilion and has 265 live oak and cypress tree shaded acres. And a thriving casino. The Coushatta is too small and too far away. They've discussed the possibility of expanding tribal acreage. The government has expanded American Indian territories in the past. However, a big sticking point is that Indian treaties don't extend to people who aren't American Indian. So we'd have to rewrite a few laws."

"This property is isolated," Mary said. "Why can't we stay here? Perhaps if the hearing committee sees that our community works, they would buy property for polyploids in other states."

"I could argue your point if it comes to that," Terrill said. "They can't require Indians to give up their land to polyploids either. But they could establish new polyploid reservations."

"Sorry to interrupt, Senator," Val said. "We promised to start the meeting at one o'clock. Can we discuss this a little later?"

"Of course. I'm curious about your meeting."

Mary stood. She introduced the senator, describing him as a friend of polyploids and a member of the Senate committee, which would soon schedule hearing dates concerning polyploids.

Val was relieved that he didn't want to address the group. The polyploids were enjoying the positive mood of the day. Why ruin it?

Jon brought Mary a very large easel with their goals enumerated on butcher paper.

1. *Survey land for building sites*
2. *Infrastructure: utilities, water, roads, and internet*
3. *Home/building construction*
4. *Expand agriculture for community use and income*

"These are some of our immediate goals," Mary said. "Does anyone have questions or want to add anything?"

A dark handsome man stood. "Where will we get these building materials, and who'll pay for them?"

"Good question," Mary said. "Here are a few options. We could sell lots for home sites, and you could build your own homes. We could build the homes, the trust I mean, and rent them out. Or some variation of the first two. I'd like us to decide what will work best for everyone. We want everyone to have a place to live."

"My name is Lisa Morton, a sociologist at the university." A blond woman stood. "I'd like to lend my experience in urban planning."

Hank got up from his rocking chair on the porch. "There are plenty of old farmhouses and barns made of that durable cypress wood scattered around this area. The owners would probably be glad to give you the lumber if you'd tear 'em down. I can look around and talk to people if you want me to."

"Thank you, Grandpa. For those who don't know, Hank Smythe, my adopted grandfather, lives nearby and farms rice and crawfish."

"Shouldn't we have a time frame for building? My name is Martha DeRouen. I'm expecting a baby in about a month and a half. Since my baby was conceived through parthenogenesis, I feel like it belongs to all of us and needs our communal care." Val noticed the biologists craning to see Martha. "There are three others pregnant with parthenogenetic babies, and I'm speaking for them too."

Another pregnant woman stood. "I agree. The whole community needs to help us with our babies. Most polyploid girls have boyfriends, and some call them husbands. But some of us don't have husbands to help us raise our babies. And I'll admit that I'm afraid of parthenogenesis and what's happening to us."

"May I say something about parthenogenesis, Mary?" Val said. "We know, or think we know, that all the New York and Los Angeles girls bore parthenogenetic babies at the age of seven. So far, only four of the twenty-five polyploid girls in Louisiana have conceived through parthenogenesis. We really don't know if other girls here will become pregnant."

Several people murmured agreement.

Val continued. "The four pregnant girls weren't at the meeting of Louisiana polyploids early this year. Is it a coincidence that they are the ones who are pregnant? We don't know. But my colleagues in our recently formed Department of Polyploid Studies are working on this conundrum. You can help us understand what's happening by sharing any information you can."

A polyploid boy with a dark complexion and deep brown eyes stood and said angrily, "I'm Maurice Arceneaux, and I don't think it's right that Mary and her trust get to keep Dr. Solven's assets just because he's her biological father. And I'm not the only one who feels this way." His fists clenched at his sides. "He fathered all of us as an experiment and then abandoned us to fend for ourselves among hostile people. As I see it, we can't survive without this community. He owes us, and I say we use his money to build the community. We will contribute our sweat, but his money is as much ours as it is yours."

Mary was surprised. She looked at Val, who said, "I think Maurice has a point."

"You bet I do," Maurice said.

"Maurice," Mary said, "I need to think this over."

"Sure, but we'll have to postpone any building plans until you decide."

Val now standing beside Mary said privately, "Mary, I don't think we have a choice. If we don't have the support of the other polyploids, and who knows how many agree with Maurice, we could be left with no alternative besides being sent to a reservation."

"I have a comment, Mary," Terrill said. "If your father's money is to be shared among all the polyploids he created, the number is more than 50, isn't it? I understand that he created polyploids all over the world. Val, you must know how many there are."

"Yes, Senator, the number is well over that and growing. I'll have to look at my notes." Val reached into her brief case for the manila file folder she'd thought to bring at the last minute. She quickly pulled out her notes from Dr Solven's manuscript.

"Dr. Solven created 295 polyploids in the U.S., and 50 have children by parthenogenesis. In North Korea and Russia, he created 255. They're twelve to fifteen years old by now, the oldest being in North Korea. The number of parthenogenetic babies born in North Korea and Russia is unknown, so excluding those, the number totals 600." Val sat down to let the number soak in.

Stunned silence followed Val's statistics. Then several people spoke at once, but no one, not even Maurice, claimed to have a solution. The need would overwhelm Mary's inheritance unless they could find a way to make money. Val, confused, wondered why Terrill had stirred up this bees nest.

Mary, who had listened patiently to the noisy debate, waved her arms now for silence. "I suggest we share equally here. We'll build our community with everyone contributing labor and expertise as best they can. The trust will supply the initial funding, and we'll all work together to keep things going. Our shared knowledge and experience will be more important than money."

Mary's decision seemed to satisfy everyone, at least for now. Val could imagine the kinds of problems that were looming for the community. Still, solving one problem at a time was the way she liked to do research, and this was becoming the most unusual research she'd ever been a part of.

By late afternoon, three school buses loaded with Texas polyploids arrived. Bob drove the lead bus. Mary ran to meet him.

"We left Houston at five this morning," Bob reported. "We brought 50 polyploid children! They're growing so fast Houston isn't safe for them now."

"Welcome to Polysomia," Mary greeted them.

She recognized the two other drivers as Dr. Bradley and a nurse from the clinic. This was a pleasant surprise.

The nurse said, "Mary? I'm Doris Bender." She extended her hand. "Texas Rangers forced Dr. Bradley and me to help break up the fertility lab, as you know, since you had to be notified. Then, we were blackballed from our professions, unofficially, of course. We'd like to work here in your community if that's possible. I don't have a family, so there's just one of me." She ran her hand over her buzzed blond hair and shifted nervously from foot to foot as she talked.

"I have a wife and two children, but we could live in Arath if you don't have room for us here," Dr. Bradley said. "I can provide medical care for your community, although with your regeneration genes, who knows? I might not be that necessary."

Four days later, the community of polyploids and helpers had finished the cafeteria construction and furnished the building with appliances and cookware. Although many of the community still lived in tents, everyone seemed happy to be working and seeing the community grow.

XXXX

Trouble began Friday night after supper, as the loud noise of trucks approaching the house penetrated Mary's sleep like a bad dream. She and Jon sprang from bed and ran to the porch in time to see at least twenty men jump from pick-up trucks. They doused gasoline onto long torches.

"Burn 'em," someone yelled as the young Texans streamed out of their tents. They were startled by the fire but quickly recovered and took action. They were larger and stronger and easily overpowered the men. But it was too late to save the tents which had completely burned, leaving only their scorched metal frames.

"I'll call the police," Jon said.

"That's real funny. We are the police." One of the men belched. "We're the Swamp Rat Vigilante Enforcement aimin' to rid our territory of you inhumans, you freaks!"

"Why are you doing this?" Jon asked. "We're not bothering you."

"Everybody knows who you are and where you are. You're

man-made! And if you get your way, you freaks will try to run this country. But we aren't going to let you. You're an abomination, born of sinful acts, Father Landry says. God says."

"Encouraging acts of hate doesn't sound like God to me," Jon said. "I'm still calling the police."

"Look, ya dumb bastard. I'm the police chief in Arath, so put the phone back in your pocket. We'll go now." He shook himself loose from the polyploid holding him. "But we'll be back. You've got three days to get out before we burn down everything else y'all got here."

"Let them go," Jon said, gritting his teeth.

Mary waited until morning to call Val to tell her about the vigilantes. "Is there an authority over the local police? What about the sheriff?" Mary asked.

"Unfortunately, I suspect others in parish law enforcement might be involved as well," Val said. "I know about Father Landry's radio broadcasts. He's inciting everyone against the polyploids on religious grounds."

"What about the FBI? Surely they don't approve of the vigilante activities of law enforcement officers," Mary said.

She was not feeling especially optimistic when she went to the community breakfast. She waited until most had finished eating before standing up. "We need to talk about what happened last night, and we need to protect ourselves from the next attack."

"We could build a solar-powered alarm system around the perimeter of the property," Paul said.

"Good, Paul," Jon said. "We need to post guards around the clock."

Jon scheduled several of the largest male polyploids, including himself, to guard the perimeter of the property. By their deadline, the guards and alarm system were ready. The polyploids were vigilant as darkness descended.

They heard the trucks as they approached the main entrance into Polysomia. But they didn't keep coming. Jon and several others went to investigate and found numerous black SUVs with FBI logos stamped on the doors blocking the Polysomia property. Reluctantly, the Swamp Rats got back into their trucks and drove away.

CHAPTER 10

Monday morning, Father Landry parked in front of the WPXU radio station to record his twenty-minute sermon. His growing corpulence made the effort of emerging from the car more and more difficult. As usual, he wore his black cassock with matching satin buttons and piping around the neck. The black contrasted sharply with the clerical tab collar. Some lay people, especially non-Romans, might have considered his dress effeminate. He could have worn the more common attire for street wear: pants and shirt with a clerical collar, but he felt people were more reverential toward him in his cassock. Even though only the tips of his black shoes showed, he polished them to a high gloss.

"Hello Father," a parishioner greeted him. He responded with a perfunctory "Bless you." His parish was the largest outside of New Orleans with over three thousand members. Surely, he couldn't be expected to know all of their names. His associates, four other priests, shared the duties of daily Communion and Sunday masses with him. Their help made it possible for him to travel and study without concern.

His favorite trips were to Thailand. He told his associates that his destination was nearby Australia because of Thailand's decadent reputation, and it was true that his plane stopped over Australia. The Vegas advertisement could just as well be used for Thailand: "Whatever happens in Thailand, stays in Thailand." He wished he'd left the DVDs in Thailand that he'd smuggled out for his university friends on his last trip.

He walked directly to the studio, continuing to acknowledge greetings along the way with "Bless you." The studio had been readied for him to use. The soundman set up the sound system to make the technology transparent to Landry. He needed only the pages of his sermon and a microphone; the rest was done for him.

He fretted that the chair in front of the microphone would

break, as several had collapsed before. On signal from the sound technician, he began to speak. The sermon was the one he had read from the pulpit the day before. The ears he wanted to reach failed to darken the doors of the church. His message was about the menace and abomination of polyploids multiplying among them.

Good morning, my people. I want to talk to you today about a growing menace. Giants! Canaanites! Polyploids! That menace we all know from Genesis. The great saints and early church fathers warned us about antichrists among us long ago. These giants are not like us. You've seen them in the news, that murderer and insane Canaanite, Michael Pitre, the worst of them. But they are all ungodly.

Many of you know that Michael attended St. Joseph's Church here in Vermilion, where I am rector. I knew him well. His parents insisted that he take catechism, and after two classes, I was forced to expel him. He openly denied Christ and asked that I prove the resurrection occurred. He said he believed that Christ's crucifixion was no more than murder. At only four years old, he was as mature as any man and calling everything we believe in into question.

St. John and St. Paul warned about the many antichrists of their time and the Antichrist to come. When the polyploid, Michael Pitre, denied Jesus is Christ, he proved himself to be among the antichrists.

Evil attains its greatest heights by simulating good things that fascinate us. Michael and the other polyploids fascinate us with their size alone, don't they? Our early church fathers recognized that signs, marvels, and counterfeit miracles come from the devil, the father of the antichrist. John describes antichrists as beasts who are against Christ. Aren't the polyploids beast-like?

Polyploids are marvels in themselves? The signs and lying miracles are there for anyone to see. They achieve adulthood at an age when the rest of us are entering first grade. Their super intelligence is a marvel and miracle. I've heard that they read books at college level and do advanced mathematics by the time they're six years old. Aren't those the marvels of antichrists?

Counterfeit miracles that the early church fathers warned us about are clear in the very conception of these beasts. They're created in Petri dishes by a doctor and then implanted to grow inside normal women. Rumors abound that the fetus grows so rapidly, pregnancy lasts only three months. Isn't that an evil marvel?

One of our early church fathers wrote that the fall of the Roman Empire made way for the antichrist. Continuing with his prediction, I say that the fall of the world economy, led by our own United States in recent years, reveals the antichrist among us. I predict that the fruition of an antichrist movement throughout the world is the artificially created polyploid race. It's with great trepidation that I give you this evidence of the rise of evil that perhaps began with the fall of the Roman Empire.

I have only one recommendation to help us curtail this rise of evil, and that is to beware. Don't be taken in by your natural human desire to love them as if they were human. They are manifesting marvels and counterfeit miracles described by the saints as characteristic of antichrists. You must do all in your power to defeat them, regardless of their beguiling evil genius.

Several of the radio station staff had gathered to listen to Landry and smirked at first at his message. But by the end of his sermon, they were nodding agreement.

I want to remind you of the blog that the polyploid daughter of Dr. Solven started. Dr. Solven is the person who created the polyploids. The title of the blog in itself was offensive, "News of the Polyploid Race: Homo sapiens *subspecies* polysomiens.*" They call themselves a new subspecies. The antichrists would think themselves superior and new, wouldn't they?*

I have learned from the antichrist's website, now removed suspiciously, that Dr. Solven created polyploids in North Korea and Russia before coming to the U.S. to do the same. Does that remind you of the new kingdoms that emerged after the fall of the Roman Empire? Today, from the ashes of the current world economic collapse, Asia, of which North Korea is a part, and Russia will certainly be included in the new kingdoms of the antichrist. That the polyploids were first created in those places is a sign like those the early church fathers warned us about. Beware, my friends.

That concludes my message for the week. Thank you for listening. May God bless and protect you all.

Landry rose from his wobbly chair and opened the door to the studio. The station staff greeted him with applause and inundated him with questions. He answered by saying, "Come to St. Joseph's next week to hear more."

Then he left the studio and drove back to the rectory. The cook had prepared breakfast for the priests, and the aroma of the food encouraged Landry's appetite, despite the many leftover biscuits with fig preserves he'd eaten at six o'clock that morning before going to WPXU. His favorite fig preserves had been made of fruit from trees on the rectory grounds, and of course, sugar from local growers. There should be a festival to bless and celebrate figs like there was for sugarcane, he daydreamed before joining the other priests in the dining room, where they had a visitor.

"Hello, I'm Congressman Reginald Migues. I didn't expect to get breakfast, but they insisted," he said, gesturing to the other priests at the table with his hand. "I hope you don't mind, Father Landry. I'm a member of St. Luke's parish in Delcambre."

Landry shook his hand and said, "You're welcome at our table." In truth, he resented sharing food, even with the other priests. "Is this a business call?"

"Yes, I guess you could call it that. I've been listening to your radio messages about the polyploid menace and wanted to thank you, personally, for your courage in speaking out. We need to do something before it's too late. At the national level, action is being taken with a Senate hearing that will be announced soon. But as a Louisiana legislator, I think we need to marshal forces against these creatures at the state level."

"I agree with you," Landry replied. He didn't like talking business while he ate. Discourse at the table disturbed the sensual pleasure of eating. "Let's talk about this in my office after breakfast, Congressman. Please pass the fig preserves."

After breakfast, he escorted Migues to his office down the hall and took a seat in the oversized burgundy leather chair behind his desk. He offered Migues the matching winged chair and invited him to continue the conversation.

Migues said, "Dr. Solven's daughter, Mary, bought a farmhouse and a thousand acres in my parish within spitting distance of Delcambre. She's openly living with Jon Landry, a polyploid she calls her husband. Landry. You have the same family name. Is he in any way related to you?"

"He was birthed through IVF by my brother's wife. However, I don't consider polyploids to be human, and I am. So, no. We're not related," Landry rose from his chair as if to dismiss Migues.

"OK, sorry I asked. Forget it. I'll get back to the reason I wanted to talk to you." Migues realized he'd angered Landry.

Landry sat back in his chair and waited for Migues to continue.

"My people in Delcambre don't like being exposed to immoral polyploid behavior, evil genius, and physical strength. I learned from reading her blog that they're building a village, and my sources say they've been joined by a bunch of Texas polyploids. A group of citizens from Arath tried to scare them off and managed to burn down the big tents they're using for temporary living quarters."

"That's good news, Congressman. I'm glad my efforts have stirred people to act. These man-made creatures are abominations under heaven, wantonly flaunting their sexuality. Suppose our children performed sex acts at six years old. That's the example the polyploids set for them. And of course, TV news eagerly exploits their sexual precocity."

"I agree, Father. But what can we do at the state level?"

"What about the Louisiana National Guard? Can't the governor use them to disperse the polyploids?" Landry tried but failed to suppress a large burp.

"I think the governor might be persuaded if he feels enough pressure from his constituents. But if the church got behind us on the polyploid issue it would help. If bishops in New York, California, and Texas join in, we might even get the attention of the Pope."

Landry's ears perked up. If he could bring the attention of the Pope to his parish for any reason, his career would skyrocket.

Migues continued. "Do you think the Pope might speak out? I know it's largely an American problem, but still."

"It's true," Landry said. "Polyploids are an American problem. But they exist in North Korea and Russia. The Roman Catholic faith is small in Russia and nonexistent in North Korea. However, the practices of deviant sexuality are prominent in the Pope's mind lately. For good reason. Perhaps he could be persuaded to make a statement. Maybe not an encyclical, but something."

CHAPTER 11

Val booked rooms for herself, David, Mary, and Jon at the Capitol Hill Suites a few blocks from the Capitol. The connecting flight from New Orleans arrived at Ronald Reagan National Airport at four p.m. From there, they took the Metro, which brought them within an easy walk to their hotel. Under other circumstances, they would have enjoyed the sights of the nation's capitol, but they felt uprooted, victimized.

The hearing before the Investigative Subcommittee of the U.S. Senate Committee on Homeland Security and Governmental Affairs was set for Monday, April 6, in the Cannon House Building. Witnesses had been invited, and subpoenaed materials had been sent to Senator John Nolan, a Republican from Georgia appointed to head the committee. Subpoenaed items consisted of Solven's manuscript and journals, boxes of clinic records, and copies of birth certificates for Mary and Jon. Fifteen members were appointed. Many represented states where the religious right and Tea Baggers were strong. Zealots preaching from the pulpit had begun to call openly for the elimination of "this man-made race of humans," decrying them as the "work of the devil."

The witnesses, Val, David, Mary, Jon, Jon's parents, Tom Bradley, and the Pitres, sat at a long table facing the committee: Chairman Nolan, a dozen male senators in dark suits, and three female senators dressed in high style. Several aides clustered behind each Senator.

Camera lenses zoomed in on Nolan's face, as he addressed the group. "This committee has been appointed to investigate the polyploids," Nolan said. "Our intention is to understand what they are, how they are different from us, what dangers they might pose to society at large, and what if necessary we should do about them. Ultimately, we aim to evaluate the consequences of their continued presence among normal people." Cameras flashed incessantly while he spoke. Videos recorded expressions of the panel, witnesses, and audience.

"We'll begin by questioning the polyploids and their family members. In the first round, each member of the committee will be given fifteen minutes. We'll have as many rounds as necessary. I'll begin with a question for Mary Solven. Ms. Solven, are you a polyploid?"

"Yes," Mary said.

"How old are you?"

"Seven years old."

"That's accurate according to the year given on the copy of your birth certificate I have here before me," Nolan said. "And do you have a child, Mary?"

"Yes, I have a baby boy."

"Who's the father?"

"Jon Landry is his father, and he's sitting here beside me."

"When was your baby born, and approximately when was he conceived?"

"He was born seven months ago and conceived three months prior to that," Mary said.

"Really? That means you could have four babies every year," Nolan said, grinning at Mary. "Are you married to this Jon Landry?" The deep octave of his voice vibrated the air.

"No, we aren't legally married. We're not old enough," she said.

"Well, no. The law doesn't apply to you and those like you, does it?"

Val knew Nolan was trying to bait Mary.

But Nolan stopped suddenly. "That's all I have to ask at the moment. I believe Senator Smith has a few questions."

"Let's get back to the marriage business, Ms. Solven," Smith said. The streaks of gray in his black hair glinted in the light of the hearing room. "Maybe you want to reconsider your answer to Senator Nolan's question about marriage. I seem to remember seeing pictures of you in a wedding ceremony on TV."

"I answered his question truthfully. I'm not legally married," Mary answered.

"But because of your backyard marriage ceremony you consider yourself to be married, don't you, Ms. Solven?" Smith didn't wait for her to answer. "You notice that I said Ms. Solven and not Mrs. Landry because you're not married in my eyes or in the eyes of God. You're not so special that you can alter the family values decent people uphold in this beloved country of ours, can you?"

Smith seemed unable to contain his anger, but Val suspected the drama was for his constituents. The hearing would have been more objective without the cameras.

"I also have a few questions for Mrs. Chris Landry. Tell me, Mrs. Landry, what do they do at the Solven Fertility Clinic? And why would a decent woman like you go there?"

He can't be serious, Val thought. He must know what fertility clinics do? You'd think they were whorehouses.

"I wanted to have a baby," Chris said. "And my husband and I couldn't do that by ourselves."

"You needed instruction?" Smith laughed at his joke.

"No, we didn't go there for instructions. We used *in vitro* fertilization. First I had to provide an egg, so—"

"That's your son, isn't it?" Smith interrupted, pointing at Jon. "Did you bear that freak in just three months too?"

"Senator Smith, I ask you to be civil to the witnesses, please," Nolan said. "You may answer the question, Mrs. Landry."

"I carried my son, Jon, for three months before he was delivered at the clinic by Dr. Solven. And I resent you calling him a freak!"

"That's enough, Mrs. Landry. I apologize for Senator Smith. Let's keep this hearing civil, Senators," Nolan said. "Your time is up, Senator Smith. Senator Langford, do you have any questions?"

Senator Langford, a woman of about forty-five, dressed impeccably in an ivory suit, asked, "Mrs. Landry, was Dr. Solven surprised at your premature delivery?"

"No, he said that was normal at his clinic."

"Did you continue to take Jon to the clinic for pediatric care?"

"The clinic doesn't have pediatricians, and Jon was never sick," Chris said.

"Describe Jon's boyhood for the committee. Was his development normal? Did he play with other children?"

"Jon was a wonderful child, but he grew up too fast. I hardly had time to hold him as a baby. I couldn't have asked for a better-behaved child. He walked at four months and grew taller every day. By the time he was five, he had become a very tall man. Not as tall as now but still tall for most men." Chris answered as if she were confessing to a priest. But she'd get no absolution from this committee, Val thought.

"What about schooling and socializing with other children?" Langford asked.

"He looked like an adult by the time he was pre-school age, so I couldn't send him to school. Besides, he'd taught himself to read, do math, and write by the time he was two years old. He's read thousands of books. He's especially interested in science."

"Your allotted minutes are up, Senator Langford." Nolan stepped in. "Senator Beadle, you're next."

Beadle twirled his pen like a cheerleader with a miniature baton before speaking. "He sounds like a prodigy. But if, as Mary Solven said, he's the father of her child, then he's not too smart about some things, is he, Mrs. Landry?"

Abruptly, he turned to Jon. "Mr. Landry, what do you have to say about impregnating Ms. Solven at age seven, or so you say? Is it the intention of polyploids to reproduce rapidly?"

"We fell in love. We were alone together for a couple of nights, and it just happened."

"Who left you alone?" Beadle asked.

"Dr. Solven. We stayed in his house in Houston. We drank a bottle of wine at dinner, and Bob drove us home afterwards. We love each other. I know it was stupid of us not to use contraception, but we weren't thinking clearly."

"I think that's enough detail, Mr. Landry. We get the picture. Tell me, why would Dr. Solven give you a bottle of wine and then leave you alone together?" Beadle didn't wait for Jon to answer. "In my opinion, he knew very well what would happen when he threw two randy polyploids together. He planned everything to perpetuate his beloved polyploids." He spat the words. "I only wish he were here to account for what he's done. That's all I have for now, Senator Nolan."

"Senator Turner, you're next," Nolan announced.

"I have some questions for Dr. Smythe. According to Dr. Solven's notes, he built a fertility clinic in New York after he arrived from Russia. Then he left there and built one in Los Angeles, Vermilion, and in Houston, where he died. I understand you're the head of a new department studying polyploids at your university in Louisiana. Since the name of your department isn't the Department of *Louisiana* Polyploid Studies, I assume you've tried to find polyploids in other states and countries." Turner chuckled at his cleverness. "What have you found, Dr. Smythe?"

"My department is barely six months old, and I've only recently selected the faculty. The case of Michael Pitre in Houston has taken much of my time." She hoped her stonewalling wasn't evident. The names of the parents of polyploids were in Solven's files, so why didn't they call them as witnesses?

"Oh, yes," Turner said, "Michael Pitre, who was charged with killing Dr. Solven and unable to stand trial because of his insanity. Another evil side of polyploidy—murderous violence, besides wanton sexuality and proliferation, starting at a young age. You still haven't answered my question, Dr. Smythe. Polyploids from out of state?"

"I think the arrest of Michael Pitre put the Louisiana polyploids in the spotlight." Val hoped the non sequitur would go unnoticed.

"By my calculations, New York polyploids should be a minimum of ten years of age, the Los Angeles, eight, and Texas, one." Turner had the eyes of a firebrand preacher.

"Yes, that's right," she said. It was clear he'd done his homework.

"We will need you to provide us with their names and addresses," Turner commanded.

"The names of the parents of polyploids are in Dr. Solven's files subpoenaed by this committee, Senator Turner," she answered.

"She's right, Senator Turner, we have that information. What are you driving at?" Nolan said, his face and bald spot turning red.

"Yes, but she's being investigated also, Senator Nolan, and we should expect her to cooperate with us," Turner said.

"Very well. Continue," Nolan said.

"Thank you, Senator. Dr. Smythe, it's audacious of you and your university to legitimize these man-made creatures by devoting a department to studying them. *Creature* is the right word for them. According to Dr. Solven's writing, he put genes for parthenogenesis from another animal into them. I'm not a doctor, so that's my paraphrasing of his words. Did you read that part of his manuscript, Dr. Smythe?"

"Yes," Val answered slowly, realizing that he had read the manuscript.

"What is parthenogenesis, Dr. Smythe?" Turner asked. "Please explain in terms all of us here can understand."

"Parthenogenesis is a type of asexual reproduction. It means the female conceives without sexual union."

"I see. In other words, these females can make babies all by themselves without intercourse with a man. Is that what you mean, Dr. Smythe?"

"Yes." She swallowed back the sour taste of bile that rose from her stomach to the back of her throat. She knew what the next question would be before he asked and wished she could lie.

"Do you know of any pregnant virgin polyploids?"

"Yes, I do," Val answered.

"What are their names? Remember, you're under oath, Dr. Smythe."

"Very well. Martha Derouen, Nancy Girouard, Gloria Breaux, and Karla Jones."

"Senator Nolan, I want them examined by gynecologists," Turner said. "I don't believe this parthenogenesis story."

"I'll appoint a gynecologist in Louisiana. After he examines the women, I'll call him to testify," Nolan said. "And Dr. Smythe, please give my assistant the information we need to get in touch with these four women."

XXXV

On the way back to the hotel, Val stopped at a newsstand to buy the *Washington Post*. The front page featured Mary and Jon's picture and an article about the hearings entitled "Giants Arrive in D.C. to Testify."

Once again, Val thought, everything is moving too quickly. Why can't they just leave Mary and Jon alone?

They stayed in their rooms and ordered lunch. An hour later they walked back to the capitol for the afternoon session. A small crowd of demonstrators carrying derogatory banners met them on the steps of Cannon House Building. Everyone seemed to be part of a group. Normal People Against Deviants, Families For Diploid Freedom, and even Greens Against Giants. Their concerns were simple. Giants used more resources than normal people, and their rapid population growth would make the achievement of sustainability impossible. Throughout the United States, conservatives protested that taxpayers were paying dearly for the cost of the hearings.

Back in the committee room, Nolan asked Senator Thomas if he had any questions.

Thomas spread the wings of his black bow tie with his thumb and forefinger before replying, "I sure do, and they're for Dr. Smythe. We know that you've been in contact with polyploids for quite some time—in New York, Los Angeles, Houston, and Louisiana. Have any of those girls borne children by parthenogenesis?"

"Yes, they have," Val said.

"How many of these children are there?"

"Fifty," Val said.

"Fifty! That's incredible! You've been withholding information, Dr. Smythe. We could have you arrested right now. You're helping proliferate a menace to mankind." Thomas' pale eyes bulged as he admonished her. "Dr. Solven says in his book that he created 550 polyploids worldwide. In the U.S., alone, he created 295. These freaks are super smart. Everyone knows about North Korea's nuclear weapons. Are they helping Koreans build these to conquer the world, Dr. Smythe?"

"Polyploids are peaceful people, Senator Thomas," Val said, hoping he wouldn't mention Michael.

"Then I have another question, Dr. Smythe, one more in your line than international politics. Where did Dr. Solven get the genes for parthenogenesis that he put in the polyploids?"

"According to his notes, they're roundworm genes," Val answered. The committee members and audience began talking among themselves. Didn't they know this already? They had his writings.

"What is the work called where a scientist puts genes of one species into another, Dr. Smythe?" Thomas asked.

"Transgenic engineering," she answered.

"I think it's sinful to put genes from animals into people. That's meddling with God's creation, and we're going to be punished if we don't stop it. Do you have anything to say about that, Dr. Smythe?" Thomas scornfully emphasized her title, Doctor.

"I don't begin to know what God thinks," Val answered.

"You will soon enough." Thomas glared at her, and judging from the whispers audible to Val, members of the committee seemed to agree. "What are these children like who come from parthenogenesis, Dr. Smythe?"

"They're like their mothers," Val said.

"What do you mean *like* their mothers?" Thomas asked.

"I mean they're genetically identical to their mother," Val said.

"You mean they're clones. Isn't that right, Dr. Smythe?"

"Yes."

"As if early and short pregnancy by normal sexuality weren't enough! And I use the word normal loosely. But now polyploid mothers can make clones of themselves like roundworms. Have you ever dug up a shovelful of fertile dirt? The number of worms in just one shovelful is amazing, Dr. Smythe. Just imagine what we'd have if these worms were giants."

"I'm afraid I must interrupt the hearing," Nolan said. "I just got a message that we're expected in the Senate chamber for an important vote. This hearing is adjourned until tomorrow morning at ten o'clock." He banged his gavel.

Back in the hotel, Mary and Jon took turns surfing cable news stations and found they were the news of the hour. Religious leaders, scientists, ranchers, businessmen—everyone had an opinion. And most of them had a problem with the polyploids.

Father Landry said the giants were a manifestation of evil. Environmentalists speculated that the potential growth rate of the polyploids through parthenogenesis could lead to a population explosion. Ranchers were concerned the giants would be relegated to the thousands of acres of protected public lands that they relied on to raise beef.

XXXX

"Dr. Bradford," Senator Fuller said. "You worked in the Solven Fertility Clinic in Texas as a gynecologist. What can you tell us about how Dr. Solven created these polyploid babies?"

"If you mean, can I explain Dr. Solven's work, then I can't. He was a genius."

"Surely you must know what he did in the laboratory. You worked with him," Senator Fuller said.

"Yes, of course. I helped with some of the experiments. We needed a way to double the number of chromosomes in fertilized eggs. Human sperm and ova have only one set of chromosomes. Researchers in North Korea discovered that fertilized ova of mice, bathed in a solution that included a diluted herbicide, would grow into embryos with double the normal number of mice chromosomes."

"Do you mean these babies were grown using herbicides?" Fuller said, raising his voice.

"Not exactly. Or yes, that's part of the equation. Dr. Solven put ova and sperm together, and fertilization occurred as in any *in vitro* fertilization. The new cells that formed are called zygotes. He then treated these zygotes with an herbicide that induced them to double in chromosome number before the first cell division."

"And then, like bad seeds, he planted these in mothers. Is that about right, doctor?"

"No. Not bad seeds. Just different seeds."

"And can another scientist with expert knowledge like you duplicate these seeds?"

"Yes, of course. But you'd need a sophisticated laboratory, and there's quite a bit more to it than I've told you. Everything—the quantities and qualities of chemicals, timing, catalysts, and so on. And Dr. Solven kept some of the equations to himself."

"To himself?"

"Yes. That's not unusual, especially for a genius like him."

"So where are these special equations?

"I can't answer that. Because I don't know."

Senator Jones said with a Boston accent, "Dr. Bradford, it's my understanding that fertility clinics make extra embryos to use in case the original implants don't take. These are usually stored unless parents give permission for their destruction. I read the other day that there were over four hundred thousand embryos stored in fertility clinics in the United States. Imagine if even a fraction of these were polyploid and got implanted behind our backs."

"Yes, I see your point," Dr. Bradford said. "Fertility clinics do store extra embryos for later use, if necessary."

"What happened to those polyploid embryos stored at the Solven clinic, Dr. Bradford?"

"They were destroyed, Senator. I destroyed them," Bradford said.

"Ah, very good!" Jones said. "Then I have one more question. Do you think polyploids are human? Fully human, I mean. If not, then perhaps they should be considered a new species?"

"That's not my area of expertise. Perhaps you should ask Dr. Smythe that question."

"I'll do that. Dr. Smythe?"

"Well," Val began slowly, "if individuals interbreed and produce fertile offspring that resemble their parents, then we'd say they were the same species. But some humans are sterile, so are they a different species? Others are deformed. So a definition based on the ability to interbreed is only somewhat helpful."

"I get the point, Dr. Smythe," Jones said. "Then have you heard of the subspecies *Homo sapiens polysomiens*, Dr. Smythe?"

"Yes, but it was only a name invented for a blog. The name looks scientific, but it's not legitimately recognized by biologists."

"Not recognized by you, Dr. Smythe?"

"That's open for debate," Val answered as her mind raced. If they can't interbreed with diploids, they could be named a subspecies of *Homo sapiens*, as Mary suggested in the blog, or another species of *Homo*, depending on how a biologist wanted to split hairs. But in her research with polyploid *Eupatorium* plant populations, she'd resisted describing them as new species because they were so similar to their diploid relatives. "We have no evidence concerning inter-fertility of polyploids and diploids. Until that time, I'll reserve judgment."

Her answer defied her own base of knowledge, but she had to protect the polyploids from tactics that would dehumanize them. She recalled a recent issue of *Science* that reported that one to four percent of DNA in modern people in Europe and Asia was inherited from Neanderthals, and scientists couldn't agree on their classification. Some designated them as a separate species, *Homo neanderthalensis.* Other scientists considered them a separate subspecies of man, *Homo sapiens neanderthalensis.* Interbreeding was a solution to xenophobia for Neanderthals, but what about for polyploids? It didn't seem likely.

XXYY

At breakfast in the hotel restaurant the next morning, Val, David, Mary, and Jon were surprised by Senator Terrill.

"I'm glad I caught you," he said. "No, no, please don't get up. I'll get a chair."

As they made room for him, he said, "I'm afraid I have more bad news. There's growing pressure on Congress to limit the growth of polyploid populations."

"What?" Val exclaimed.

"I mean the committee conservatives are talking forced sterilization of the females." He let that sink on. "Proof of parthenogenesis will be critical in making this decision, although I'm sure that the four pregnant girls are telling the truth."

"That's barbaric! Involuntary sterilization is illegal. That's even been outlawed for mental incompetents," Val said. She was outraged. "What about the pregnant girls? Will they have to abort their babies?"

"There's no talk of aborting babies yet," Terrill said slowly. "The conservatives don't like the word abortion, but sterilization doesn't seem to bother them as much. The committee recommendation, which will carry considerable weight in Congress, hinges on whether the committee thinks polyploids have the same rights as diploids. The consensus among them right now is that the law only applies to humans who have been 'created by God.'" Terrill paused, nervously twisting his tie designed with Tabasco sauce bottles and orange crawfish.

"Hysterectomies," he said gently, "would be the most effective control measure. They know that sterilizing male polyploids would do nothing to control parthenogenesis. So they'll probably feign compassion by saying they don't want to do anything more than what's necessary. If sterilization is recommended, they'll look for every single polyploid female in the United States. It will be hard to hide giants. The FBI already has access to your correspondence, emails, blogs. They'll hunt them down when the time comes."

XXXX

At the hearing the next morning, Nolan asked if Senator Terrill had any questions.

"Yes, thank you, Senator. I'd like to ask the committee members a few questions. First of all, do any of you think that the polyploids, Mary and Jon, look like they're another species?"

"Wait a minute, Senator Terrill, I don't think this is appropriate," Senator Beadle said, vigorously twirling his pen.

"That's right. We're here to question the witnesses, Senator," Nolan said. "Please address your questions to them."

"But Senator Nolan, it's this committee's opinion that will decide the fate of the polyploids." He paused to let the murmurings of the other committee members die down. "Then I'll ask Dr. Smythe. How much genetic difference is there between polyploid and diploid humans?"

"The polyploid and diploid human genes differ in chromosome number, but otherwise they're genetically identical." Val stretched the truth, ignoring the inserted genes.

"Well that seems simple enough. If they have the same genes, aren't they the same? But how about in other species, what does this duplication of chromosomes do?"

"Polyploidy in other species influences size, robustness, vigor, and stress resistance. Polyploidy in itself provides more genetic output, so to speak. In theory, the more copies of a gene, the more DNA is available, and the more it can do. Enzymes involved in the making of proteins are perhaps the best understood part of what DNA does. There's also dark matter, which regulates genetic function. But that's more complicated. In general, if you compare the amount of a certain enzyme from both a polyploid and a diploid organism, the polyploid will likely produce more of that enzyme."

"Very interesting," Senator Terrill said. "In your research with plants, do you advocate that the polyploids be recognized as new species?"

How did he know so much about her research? She said, "In the plants I study, some individuals are polyploid. They're larger and more vigorous than the diploids. Otherwise, they're identical. So no, I don't recognize them as separate species."

She left it at that. But unlike human polyploids, the plants were totally parthenogenetic with no sexual reproduction that she knew about.

"Then can you think of any reason polyploid humans should be treated differently from diploid humans?"

"No, I can't."

"What do you have to say about that, Mary?" he turned toward her, a giant who had been strangely ignored throughout the questioning. And Mary was startled at being recognized.

"Well, our feelings and desires to live a productive and peaceful life are no different from anyone's. We know we're different. We grow faster. We mature faster. But that's not our fault. We can't change the way we are."

"Your time is up, Senator Terrill," Senator Nolan said. "Senator Boyd, do you have any questions?"

Senator Boyd tucked a strand of blond hair behind her ear. "I'd like to bring forth a new witness to shed some light on this, from a more personal perspective you might say. Jacque Simoneaux, would you please come forward?"

"Do you know Mary Solven, Jacque?" Senator Boyd asked after

Jacque had been sworn in. "And if so, where did you meet her?"

"Yeah, I know Mary. She used to run in Gerald Park. I already told all that to the FBI."

"We want to hear how you met Mary, directly from you."

"She played pick-up with us. And I saw her at Starbuck's once. She likes lattes." Jacque tapped his foot nervously.

"Was Mary good at the pick-up game? That's basketball, right, Jacque?"

"You're right about that. I never saw anybody jump like her. And she's fast! Everyone liked to watch her. Not even runnin' full out she'd do a mile faster than anyone I ever saw. But we never timed her. Her second mama, here," he nodded toward Val, "she's just like her first mama. Didn't want her hangin' out with us, so she stopped showin' up."

"Jacque, I can tell you like sports a lot," Boyd said. "As a sports activist, do you think it would be fair for Mary to compete against normal people? Say, in the Olympics?"

"I see what you mean. It's kinda like 'roids, 'cept not even juice makes you that good. Polys need a Special Olympics. Don't get me wrong. I like polys. Me and my friends want to get engineered. Could we, Mary?" Jacque looked at Mary.

"Never mind," Boyd said. "You and your friends cannot be engineered."

CHAPTER 12

"Martin, I need some lumber to do a little building," Hank said to his friend on the phone. "I can tear down that old abandoned farmhouse you got on your property, if you give me the wood. It's gonna burn down one of these days anyway, you know." Hank figured it was better if he say who would do the tearing down. Although it wouldn't be enough, the old cypress was stronger than any new lumber they could buy, and this bartering would save money.

The Senate hearing had been bad publicity for the polyploids. So he preferred to keep them out of the conversation, although he hated lying to his friend.

"I'm thinkin' you'll have more land to plant if you git rid of them old run down buildings. I'm buildin' me a few rent houses. I'm thinkin' rent might be better than them rice and crawfish. *Mais* yeah, it's risky, but I'm gonna try it."

Unless Martin discovered polyploids doing the work, Hank could live with his deception. If Martin found out, he'd deal with the consequences. Hank made a list of six more friends with abandoned buildings on their farms. Good neighbors, they all agreed to let him have the lumber, provided he'd do the work.

Hank pulled up to the Martin farmhouse towing a long flatbed trailer with as much polyploid help as he could cram into the bed of the pick-up. Peter sat beside Hank in the cab. Two other trucks followed. Fortunately, as Hank expected, Martin didn't appear at the abandoned building far from his main house. Within a few hours, they'd torn down the building and loaded the lumber.

But things didn't go as smoothly at all the farms. James Rosier drove up as they were loading lumber at his place, and Hank could tell before he opened the door to his pick-up that he was furious. "Hank, what in hell are you doing with them freaks? You lied to me! We should run them off, not harbor them."

"James, you know my daughter, Val. She's like a mama to Mary

Solven, and Mary's like my own kin. People are doin' wrong by them. I'm sorry I wasn't straight with you. But you never woulda' gave me that lumber if I told you everything."

"Get off my land and drop that lumber where it is. I'm not helpin' any freaks. They gonna ruin us, Hank. Believe me about that. Father Landry says on the radio. I might have known about you. First thing, you marry a black and brought her here. Then, you have a mulatto daughter, and she mixes up with freaks. I see how we made us some big mistakes about you from the start."

"You making a big mistake now, James, talking about my family like that. I'm going before I teach you some truth."

Paul walked toward them, and James backed away from Hank and the pile of lumber beside the partially dismantled farmhouse.

"But first, we'll just finish what we started here," Hank said.

The pick-ups headed back to Polysomia, the trailer piled high with lumber, but a gloom overshadowed their success. Hank knew James would tell everyone how Hank had lied to them, and Hank would lose friends. But he already knew their prejudices. He'd married Belle and sired an interracial child. Anything different was the same to them. So-called friends.

Suddenly, he realized that Peter wasn't in the seat beside him. He slammed the brakes, forgetting about the trailer full of lumber in tow. The boys in the truck bed tumbled against each other.

"Where's Peter?" Hank yelled as he jumped out of the truck. We have to go back and find him."

"The last time I saw him was at the Anderson farm," Paul said. "That was a while ago."

"Let's go there," Hank said. His voice trembled with a mixture of anger at himself and fear for Peter's life. "This trailer is gonna slow me down. I'm hookin' it up to your truck, Paul. Pull it on back to Polysomia. You boys in my truck better come with me. There ain't enough room for you with the others."

After unhooking the flatbed from his trailer hitch, he sped back toward the Anderson farm, where they found Peter standing by the old farmhouse, crying, and holding a bleeding hand. Hank ran to him, impulsively sweeping him into his arms. Hank too began to cry. "Thanks be to God you safe, boy. What's the matter with your hand, Peter?"

"Grandpa, my thumb got chopped off in the middle of the proximal phalanges." Hank quickly put him down to look more closely. He ignored Peter's anatomical explanation and noticed the detached thumb Peter held in his other hand. The bleeding had stopped, but his shirt and pants were splattered with blood. Hank swallowed back the gorge that welled up from his stomach. "Does it hurt bad?"

"Not now, Grandpa. I was trying to catch a board when it fell, and my thumb flew over into a patch of tall goldenrods. I went to get it, but I bled too much. So, I sat down in the goldenrods and made a tourniquet with my belt. I found my thumb, but by that time everybody was gone."

"You gonna be fine, *cher*. We'll get that thumb put back on before you know it," Hank said. He felt like the worst human alive to have left his grandson alone and now, his thumb cut off.

Hank drove to Arath General as fast as safety allowed. Peter held his detached thumb tightly. At the hospital, Hank put his arm around Peter's shoulders, and they hurried through the emergency entrance.

"Hello, Mr. Smythe. How can I help you?" The nurse at the desk smiled at Hank, not yet noticing Peter hiding behind him. Hank pushed Peter forward.

"He needs attention now."

"Oh, my God!" she said, seeing his missing thumb. "Give me that, and I'll put it on ice until a doctor can reattach it."

When she returned she said, "What's your name?"

"Peter Solven."

Hank could tell the nurse knew the name, Solven.

"The doctor will see you right away. Wait right here. I'll be back to put you in a room."

In a nearby room she said, "Peter, I want you to lie down, and I'll put this sheet over you. Are you feeling cold, or like you might pass out?"

"No, I feel fine. Thank you, m'am. I don't think I'm in shock. I put a tourniquet on my upper arm to staunch the bleeding."

"You're such a polite young man. How old are you, Peter?" she asked. Hank cringed.

"I'm one year old," Peter replied.

"So you're four years old. What a smart, big boy you are for your age," she said. Hank hoped that Peter wouldn't correct her about his age.

"No, I'm one year old," Peter said.

"Oh, I see," the nurse said and frowned at Hank.

"I'm going to take your blood pressure and temperature, Peter," she said. She put a thermometer in his mouth and wrapped a band around his upper arm. "Blood pressure is fine, but you have a slight temperature. Have you been sick?"

"No, I feel fine," Peter said.

Dr. Clemen walked into the room and picked up Peter's chart. The nurse alerted him about the elevated temperature. "Well, young man, looks like you lost a thumb. How did that happen?"

Peter explained.

"You're a smart boy. For your age, you sure know a lot about anatomy and first aid. Where did you learn all that?"

"Dad and Mom said I needed to know about the human body. So they gave me books to read. I asked them questions, too."

Not very interested in the child prodigy, the doctor returned to considering Peter's thumb. "I'm afraid a surgeon will need to put your thumb back on. Dr. Rollins, an orthopedic surgeon, will take care of you, son."

XXYY

A few days after the operation, Peter announced to Hank that his thumb had come off again. "How do you know, *cher*?" Hank asked.

"I feel it rattling around inside the bandage," Peter said, shaking the bandaged hand.

"Let's take the bandage off and look." Hank hadn't been able to finish constructing the porch of the group home as he'd planned. First Hank, then Belle, had fallen ill with a virus.

Peter followed Hank to the kitchen where he found scissors to cut the tape.

"There it is!" Peter said. The end of his thumb lay detached, black and lifeless, on the gauze. The stitched flesh and grafted bone had sloughed away with the piece of old thumb. "Another thumb is growing. Look, Grandpa!"

Hank saw a perfect replacement for the lost part growing out of the wound of Peter's thumb. "*Cher*, I don't think we need to bother the surgeon about this anymore. Won't your mom be surprised when she gets back from D.C."

The phone rang. "Yeah. This is Hank Smythe." ... "Yeah, Peter's fine. We took the bandage off, and everything looks good." Hank winked at Peter. "His fever is gone." ... "What? A flu virus? Is that what he had? Well, he never had symptoms except the fever at the hospital." ... "He's been staying with his grandma and me while his mama's in Washington." ... "Oh, I'm sorry that Dr. Clemens and the nurse got the flu." ... "And the entire hospital staff!" ... "You know. I need to go lie down, now. Thanks for calling."

"You want some help, Grandpa?" Peter asked. "What about some orange juice? I think you need to drink lots of fluids when you have the flu. I'll bring you a glass in the bedroom."

"Yes, I am thirsty."

"I'll get some for Grandma when she wakes up," Peter said. "I'll make myself some lunch, Grandpa. So don't worry."

Hank felt dizzy. His head and joints ached. He shivered. With Peter's help, he got into bed with Belle. Peter covered them both.

When Hank and Belle woke, Peter brought scrambled eggs and toast. They ate ravenously.

"Where'd you learn to cook, Peter?" Hank asked, forking eggs into his mouth.

"Mom taught me. She said when you can reach the stove, it's time to learn to cook. Here, I brought you the newspaper."

Hank glanced at the front page. "Oh God, Belle. Peter's being blamed for spreading the flu germ throughout the hospital and into Arath."

CHAPTER 13

Under Paul's directions, the industrious group had worked furiously to try to finish the construction before Mary and Jon returned from the hearings. They had framed twenty-five buildings. So everyone had a roof, even if canvas, over their heads.

Mary walked from the farmhouse to where Martha Derouen lived with another parthenogenic pregnant girl. Martha's mother, Helen, had driven from Vermilion to Polysomia to take Martha to a gynecologist. Dr. Bradford had discreetly arranged the appointment, and Mary would accompany Martha.

"How are you feeling, Mrs. Derouen?" Mary asked as Helen got out of the car.

"I'm getting better, Mary. Still a little weak, but no more fever and aching. I'm glad that Martha didn't get this nasty flu. Reports say that polyploids are immune."

"Our immunity turns out to be another reason for diploids to resent us. Poor little Peter. He's feeling bad about spreading the flu at the hospital."

Martha walked to the car with difficulty, sobbing softly. The blue-checked maternity dress that she had sewn was tight across her belly. Mary remembered the last days before Peter's delivery when her bulging belly had impeded every move.

"Martha, the physical exam will be simple and non-invasive. Believe me. A quick look will show that your hymen is still intact." "The amniocentesis will be painful but over quickly."

"It's not the exam," Martha said, wiping her tears and pushing her dark hair from her face. "I'm angry about being ordered to prove to the world that I'm a virgin. So what, if they don't believe me? Who cares?"

"I know, I know. But we have to do this."

At the doctor's office, a nurse wearing a mask greeted them silently.

Less than an hour later, Martha returned to the waiting room. "Are you OK?" Mary asked.

"He took one quick look, just as you said he would, Mary."

"And, did he say? As if we don't know already," Mary said.

"He said, 'I'll be damned. You're a virgin.'" She looked at Mary. "Please, let's go home."

They returned to Polysomia in time for lunch, and Mary invited Helen to the cafeteria to eat with the others. Mary, with Hank's help, had been able to convince some of the poorer local people to work with them. These people, having little opportunity elsewhere, seemed happy here alongside the polyploids.

Jon arrived after everyone had sat down to eat. He waved some papers and went to Mary's table before getting his food. "Mary, look. It's mail about the GED. I made a perfect score. Here's my diploma, and this must be yours from the same address in Baton Rouge. Hurry, open it."

His excitement was contagious, and other problems temporarily forgotten, Mary opened the thin, long envelope and pulled out the unfolded pages. "I passed too! We're both high school graduates!"

"Maybe we can exempt college courses," Jon said. "I've done some research on the College Level Examination Program, which is a way to get credit for college courses. You get three to twelve credits per exam. They offer thirty-four exams, which means we could exempt the first two and part of the third year of college. The testing center is at McNeese University in Lake Charles. That's not far from here."

"Jon," Mary said, "I am so happy with us."

XXXX

Father Landry answered the phone for what seemed like the hundredth time that Tuesday. He'd recovered from the flu but had fallen behind in his work. Today he intended to respond to the collection of yellow Post-It messages that had collected on his desk. Responses to his last sermon were overwhelming.

"Yes, this is Father Landry." ... "Thank you. I'm glad you're listening. You're calling from where?" ... "California, you say. I'm syndicated nationwide, so I never know where callers are." ... "Yes, polyploids live in Los Angeles now. I know for a fact they're reproducing in abnormal ways." ... "Yes, thank you. And I've got news for them; normal people will never accept freaks. You can bank on that."

In his radio broadcast, he had made his position quite clear.

As you all know, when polyploid girls reach age seven, they become pregnant by parthenogenesis. That means that by the time they're twenty-one, the age of reason for normal people, every polyploid girl could have more than twenty children. Each of the girl children (they will all be clones of her) will become pregnant by parthenogenesis when they reach seven years old. And on it goes. We don't know what controls parthenogenetic pregnancies, but that isn't the point. Reproduction by polyploids must be stopped. Mass sterilization of all polyploid females is the answer.

Many of the callers wanted to know the church's position regarding sterilization. Of course, the Roman Catholic Church didn't condone sterilization. That wasn't the point. If Father Landry was right, that polyploids weren't human, then...

They were an unnamed, man-made species. He considered that. Strange, how synchronistic his work had become. Another reason to think God was guiding his career. He scooted his leather desk chair up to the keyboard and began to write.

I've gotten many calls concerning the ethics of sterilizing the polyploids, specifically asking me about the church's position. First, I must make it clear that I don't speak for the church. I pray for guidance and share with you my own interpretations in my broadcasts and sermons. The mistake that we make is thinking that the polyploids are human beings. They're not! They're man-made creatures. We humans were made by God and in the image of God.

We sterilize other creatures as it serves our purpose. God gave us dominion over all the earth and everything in it, including anything man-made. We're God's chosen; we began with Adam and Eve. We castrate bulls because steers fatten faster for our dinner tables. Hunters castrate wild boars so the meat will taste better. We geld stallions to make them tamer. In other words, we have good reasons for sterilizing animals.

He realized the examples were all for male animals, but his audience would get the point.

Whatever man creates, he has dominion over! That dominion includes the right to sterilize to stop their proliferation. Although they resemble us in some ways, don't be fooled. They're our competitors for food and water. They're giants!

Everyone listening now should send his or her congressman or congresswoman an email. Tell them what you think about this problem before it gets any worse. Every giant female must be sterilized!

He'd go from there. He was pleased; it would be a good sermon. Perhaps it was a little direct, but he had learned that you had to be forceful. It was for their own good. He was doing God's work. Amen.

Landry's bishop had been the first in the church's hierarchy to acknowledge his work and to offer him financial resources. Now his own parishioners were filling the church coffers with surprising amounts. The bishop suggested that Landry take his message to television, and several stations had contacted him. But he'd declined. He felt his size could detract from his mission and preferred the coziness of the radio station. He knew everybody there, and he didn't intend to give up his biscuits and fig preserves.

He was ready for a snack and had started toward his office door when his phone rang again. He stopped in mid-stride, then ignored it, continuing on to the kitchen, intent on rummaging through the rectory's institutional-sized refrigerator. He piled slices of ham on a plate, adding large dollops of mayonnaise and Dijon mustard. Half a loaf of the cook's homemade white bread would be just about right, along with a Coke.

After his snack, he went back to his office to find three new messages. The first was from a former acolyte now with the FBI, and the other two were from strangers. He dialed the FBI agent. "Hello, this is Father Landry. Sorry, I missed your call." ... "Of course I remember you. How have you been, Jim?" ... "That's great! And your sons?" ... "Wonderful." Drowsily, he endured the polite chitchat. "What's your interest in the polyploids, Jim?" ... "Yes, I know who Senator Terrill is." ... "Oh, you're halfway to Vermilion already. Well, then I'll see you soon."

Landry was just getting up from his nap when Jim arrived. He usually had a little snack after waking, but he didn't want to eat in front of Jim. Eating was a private matter, and he was particular about who he ate with.

Jim had served as acolyte until he graduated from high school and began studying criminal justice at the University of Vermilion. Although he had lived in an apartment nearby, he'd stopped attending St. Joseph's Church. Landry didn't know whether he attended mass anymore, but that wasn't his concern.

"So why do you think Senator Terrill called the FBI headquarters in D.C. about the polyploids, Jim?"

"The Swamp Rat Vigilantes from Arath raided their place one night. They burned the tents where some of the polyploids lived. The polyploids chased the vigilantes off the property before they could do much else to the place. They returned three days later, but the FBI was waiting."

Landry listened patiently, although he'd already heard about the burning from the Arath police chief.

"Dr. Val Smythe must have called Terrill, and he called the FBI. Several of us officers were ordered to stop the second raid but we weren't happy about it. It's stuck in my craw ever since. So I want your *spiritual* advice, Father. What's the right thing to do?"

This was even better than he expected. Landry put his hand to his chin as if thinking, then said, "Acting on your own would jeopardize your job, Jim, and I don't think you can do much on your own. Besides, you have to think about your family. Terrill is a member of my parish. I'll talk to him and get back to you."

Shortly after Jim left, Landry called Terrill's office. He assumed Terrill would be wary and give an excuse to call him back, but

Terrill came on the line, his congenial, non-combative greeting somewhat surprising. Liberals, thought Father Landry. They're all the same. He would be direct, forceful.

"Senator, I hear you support the polyploids, and that disturbs us here in the parish. You're out of step with your constituents, and I'd hate to see your next election campaign bloodied, so to speak, by your own views." ... "That's right, Senator, I'm a religious man." ... "Of course, this is not a threat." ... "Yes, we all have to do what we think is right, but protecting the so-called rights of polyploids is misguided." ... "You know, Senator, I have a lot of influence in Louisiana, and my nationwide audience is growing. Just say I'm advising you to be careful."

After he hung up, Father Landry turned back to his sermon.

I encourage you to tell your legislators to stop the proliferation of polyploids now. If they pretend to be uninformed about the polyploid issue, tell them to listen to my broadcasts.

That should make the point. Terrill is likely to get a lot of mail after this column comes out. He chuckled at his own cleverness.

A reminder of lunch wafted into his office, disturbing his concentration. He opened his inbox, hoping to find email from people who could help further his cause: doctors, lawyers, law enforcement officers. Ah... He opened a message from a Roman Catholic hospital in New Orleans.

Father Landry, my name is William Roemer. I'm the administrator of the Namor Hospital. I have read your columns regularly and pray daily for you in your work to save mankind from this menace. I feel called to offer our facilities and surgical staff for the polyploid sterilization procedures. Our surgeons are beginning to formulate plans to proceed whenever the time comes.

Landry was so excited he briefly forgot about lunch. He needed to contact members of the Senate committee before they reached a final decision on the polyploids. He'd call Senator Nolan first. If only there were sympathetic senators from Louisiana on the committee. Terrill was certainly not one, and he wondered what was taking them so long to make recommendations.

The buzzer announced lunch. He'd installed it in his office for quick notice that meals were ready. Communication with Senator Nolan could wait until after lunch.

When Landry returned to his desk, his appetite sated temporarily, he realized that he hadn't included the latest outrage in regard to the polyploids. How could he forget his bout with the Polyploid Flu?

He appended the new idea to the sermon.

Polyploids carry diseases to which they are immune. I've only just recovered from this dreadful disease that kept me in bed for a week. According to health officials, it started with a single polyploid boy, Peter Solven, who entered Arath General Hospital for an operation to re-attach part of his thumb. He had a slight fever, but he had no other flu symptoms. His symptoms never developed into full-blown flu. The doctor took blood and sent it to the Center for Disease Control. The CDC reported that the boy carried a flu virus strain that was new to science. We all know about the swine flu, a pandemic that swept the world last year. Well, this is a new H1N1, and there are no vaccines to prevent its spread. Somehow, this new form developed in the polyploid boy, they think. What other diseases do they harbor that can spread to humans? Isn't this even more reason to control the multiplication of polyploids?

When he was finished, he went online and found Senator Nolan's office number in D.C. A woman surprised him by saying, "Yes, Father Landry. Please hold."

Then Senator Nolan surprised him by saying he was glad he had called. One of his aides had been monitoring the Father's columns, and they were all impressed by how much he knew about polyploids.

"Thank you, Senator. And I fully support your committee's work on this issue. I like to think we're working together on this." … "Yes, yes." … "Wonderful."

This was better than Father Landry could have hoped. Senator

Nolan not only agreed with him but was eager to do something besides talk about the problem.

"Then you should know about someone here, high up I mean, at Namor Hospital in New Orleans. He said he can help us with facilities and staff for the sterilization procedures." ... "Yes, Senator, I agree. We'll have to get together some time for dinner."

XXYY

The talk in the committee room stopped when Senator Nolan hammered his gavel.

"As you know," he said, "we've been waiting for the gynecological results on the four pregnant polyploid girls who claimed to be virgins. Dr. Langlinais has sent the committee his findings. As he has verified all documents, I told him there was no need for him to appear before us in person. We now know the girls are virgins!" He let that sink in. "And DNA taken from the fetuses by amniocentesis proved identical to that of the respective mother's. The doctors, experts in this, say the girls had conceived through parthenogenesis. The fetuses are clones of their mothers."

A buzz went through the room.

"The committee began formulating conclusions in regard to the polyploid issue while waiting for these results," Nolan continued. "We, the committee, are convinced that the polyploids are not like us, which I have just shown you genetically, and pose significant risks to normal humans, or diploids, as we're called, in relation to them. Our laws, as written in the Constitution of the United States, apply to humans, not these... creatures!"

Another buzz, louder this time, went through the room.

"May I be recognized?" Senator Terrill interrupted.

"Yes, Senator," Senator Nolan pounded his gavel to quiet the audience.

"I don't agree that polyploids aren't human. They are genetically identical to us, diploid humans! And I know there are other *experts* that agree with me. The difference between diploid and polyploid humans is simply in a number, the number of chromosome sets. Therefore, the Constitution applies to them, same as us. And if man-made is another of your criteria, then keep in mind that some diploid humans have been man-made in fertility clinics. Don't they have the same rights as the rest of us diploids under the Constitution? Of course they do."

"I beg to differ, Senator Terrill," Senator Beadle interrupted. "I argued with you about this in our deliberations. I'll repeat my arguments for the public. Polyploids are not genetically identical to diploids. By no means. In addition to having double sets of chromosomes, polyploids were genetically engineered with genes from animals! They're capable of parthenogenesis, and who knows what else, because of Dr. Solven's genetic engineering. The doubling of chromosomes had the effect of making them into huge creatures with questionable intelligence and unusually early maturation. These are not normal human qualities. They are not like us, and they are dangerous. Anyone can see that."

Again, the audience was abuzz. Again, Senator Nolan pounded his gavel until silence was restored.

Then he said, "Thank you, Senator Beadle, for very succinctly stating the majority opinion."

"May I finish my argument, Senator Nolan?" Senator Terrill said.

"Yes, but make it brief. I think we're decided here."

"Diploid humans are not genetically pure either! Viruses are constantly infecting us and leaving alien genes. Viruses are nature's means of genetic engineering. *Herpes* viruses infect us and insert their genes into our chromosomes. Exposure to stress factors such as ultraviolet light activates these genes in carriers of *Herpes simplex* causing them to break out with blisters.

"Epigenetic factors also make us different genetically. They jump on our chromosomes from nowhere, it seems, and essentially control our genes, turning them off and on or changing their expression. Some epigenes cause diseases such as cancer. This is a new area of genetic study. Plainly, we have far more alien genes in us than most people know."

"That's enough, Senator," Senator Nolan said. "I think we all know your arguments by now. But it's time to let the American people know what we've decided.

"First, let me just say to all of you here and to those watching on television that the majority of the committee agrees with what I'm about to say. It's quite clear to us that parthenogenesis and early sexual maturity are threats to society. And as caretakers, you might say, of our great society, this committee can only recommend that something be done immediately to avert this threat."

"But Senator," Senator Terrill again tried to reason, "polyploids are human beings. There's genetic diversity among diploids. But we treat each other equally under the law. We don't say that people who have an extra chromosome, expressed as Down's syndrome, aren't equal under the law. Unusually tall people and short people are also treated equally under the law. In other words, divergent categories of humans aren't singled out as exceptions to the law."

"Senator Terrill," Nolan interrupted, "it's time to move on from argument. The committee is in agreement, and we have recommendations." He paused to sip from a glass. "We recommend that a treaty be established with these creatures, these polyploids. The precedent set by the treaties between the United States and American Indians should serve as our model. Our polyploid treaty, as with the American Indians, will offer generous government gifts and a peaceful life. We require only minor concessions."

He sipped. "Polyploids will be recognized as having a separate sovereign nation. The government will set aside land for them. In return for our peace offering, gifts of land and financial subsidy, the polyploids will agree not to reproduce either through parthenogenesis or normal means."

Nolan looked up from his papers.

"I want it recorded that I object to this outrage," Terrill stood to emphasize.

"Please sit down, Senator. We're civilized people here. To continue, because some of our national forests have been so devastated by fires in the past decade that they can no longer be called forests, the committee recommends that certain of these national forests be selected as polyploid reservations.

"To insure that further reproduction of polyploids doesn't occur, the committee recommends that all female polyploids be sterilized by hysterectomy, unless they're pregnant. Those females who are pregnant will undergo hysterectomies after giving birth. We're proposing to Congress that the polyploid females in Louisiana be the first to undergo hysterectomies. Let Louisiana be a model for carrying out plans in other states."

CHAPTER 14

D etective Juan Rodriguez's wife, June, had kept him awake most of the night moaning. "Labor pains," she said. "But I'll be all right. Why don't you go sleep on the couch until it's time to get up. Get a little sleep."

She didn't have to argue. He had a big day ahead of him. He got a blanket from the closet, closed the bedroom door behind him, and stretched out on the couch. He lay restless, not sleeping but thinking about how tough this pregnancy had already been. After only three months, June was as miserable now as she had been at nine before their first child.

They'd tried to have a second child and had finally given up. Then she became pregnant soon after she and Juan had recovered from the Polyploid Flu. That epidemic had begun with a polyploid boy, Peter Solven, four months before.

What a menace polyploids were.

Rodriguez woke to June's moaning.

"I'm coming," he called, then opened the door to find his wife on the floor in a small pool of blood.

"I'm OK," she managed to say, "but it's time."

Rodriguez called 911.

XXXX

"Bless me father, for I have sinned," said the woman behind the small curtain.

"How long has it been since your last confession, my child?" Father Landry asked.

"Two years, Father." She began to sob softly.

"What are your sins, my child?" Landry asked. The confessions he'd heard over the last year or so had taken on a peculiar note and had piqued his interest for the first time since he was a young priest.

"Father, I'm being punished for failing to confess my secret love for a man other than my husband." She choked back sobs.

"Have you had relations with this man?"

"No, Father. The man doesn't know. My feelings are secret, known only to me, Father, but I'm being punished for having these feelings. My sins are in my heart," she said, sounding calmer.

"How are you being punished, my child?" Father Landry knew what her answer would be from the confessions he'd heard over the past weeks.

"I've borne a child that's not normal," she replied, beginning to sob again. "My baby is beautiful, but he is growing too fast and is too smart."

The desperate confessions were always the same and rooted in superstition. A parent, usually the mother, blamed the bearing of an unusual child on sins they had been ashamed to confess, or on dark forces they attracted because of innate sinfulness. He didn't think much of their belief in superstition, but after hearing so many similar confessions, he had to conclude that the unusual children were linked to the Polyploid Flu. Like the flu itself, the unusual children had been borne in epidemic proportions, and except for their unusually short pregnancies, the women had borne normal looking children. The manifestations of their unusual nature were delayed until the children were older. Only he, Father Landry, seemed to have made the connection to the Polyploid Flu.

Before giving a blessing and suggesting a penance, he questioned this mother as he had the others.

"Have you or your husband had the Polyploid Flu?"

"Yes, Father. We both had the flu. I got pregnant just after we recovered." She was crying now. "My baby was born three months later. What's going to happen to us? Please absolve me of my sins."

"One more question before I do. Was the birth difficult for you?"

"No, Father. The baby was born at home. It came so quick I didn't have time to get to the hospital."

The answers were all the same. Both parents had recently

recovered from the Polyploid Flu. Gestation was three months, and the babies were born quickly and easily.

"Please recite the act of contrition along with me," he said leading the recitation.

> *O my God,*
> *I am heartily sorry for having offended Thee,*
> *and I detest all my sins*
> *because I dread the loss of heaven*
> *and the pains of hell,*
> *but most of all because they offend Thee, my God,*
> *Who are all good and deserving of all my love.*
> *I firmly resolve with the help of Thy grace*
> *to confess my sins, to do penance,*
> *and to amend my life.*
> *Amen.*

Father Landry responded with an absolution.

> *God the Father of mercies,*
> *through the death and resurrection of his Son,*
> *has reconciled the world to himself*
> *and sent the Holy Spirit among us*
> *for the forgiveness of sins;*
> *through the ministry of the Church*
> *may God give you pardon and peace,*
> *and I absolve you from your sins*
> *in the name of the Father, and of the Son,*
> *and of the Holy Spirit.*

As the woman left the confession box, he crossed himself. Then he returned to his office, exhausted. These confessions were starting to get to him. He needed to talk to someone, and the person who came to mind was Dr. Smythe. He knew her views, ill-advised as they were, but his curiosity outweighed his antipathy. He found her number at the university.

"Dr. Smythe, this is Father Landry, no doubt you've heard of me. I'm calling about a scientific matter, one of your research subjects."

... "Yes, the polyploids. It's a matter of unusual births, you might say. Perhaps I can come to your office, say tomorrow?"

XXXV

"How could they write this propaganda about polyploids? They don't cause influenza—viruses do," Val said to David at breakfast, referring to yet another poorly written article in the local newspaper.

"It's mass hysteria, Val. Sad, but true. Once people become afraid of something, there's nothing logical or humane about their behavior. Trying to fight them with facts is like pouring gasoline on a fire."

"But those committee recommendations were inhumane. Polyploids are walking, talking humans. Can't they see that?"

"I think they see that Mary and Jon and the others are bigger and smarter than we are. So putting them on reservations and sterilizing them is their way to feel safe without admitting they're hurting anyone."

"You mean murdering! Yeah, on reservations they're out of sight. But sterilization means they don't have a future."

"What ever happened to the proposal you and Senator Terrill were working on to let Louisiana polyploids stay in Polysomia?

"We submitted it, but I haven't heard anything." Val finished her coffee and something clicked. "David, I just remembered that I'm meeting Father Landry this morning. I'm almost certain he wants to talk about the abnormal babies born to parents that had Polyploid Flu prior to conception."

"How does he know about that?"

"I don't know. But he seems to know more about everything related to the polyploids than your average priest."

"Maybe they're confessing?"

"What?"

"The mothers. Remember, I was a priest. If you get in a tight spot, ask him about his trips to Thailand."

CHAPTER 14

XXXX

Val went straight to Walt's office, arriving just as a young couple appeared with their child. Walt's lab had become the focus of testing in recent weeks.

"Hello, I'm Allen Jordan, and this is my wife, Becky. You must be Dr. Klein," Allen said, shaking Walt's hand.

"And you're Dr. Smythe, right?" Becky offered her free hand, holding her son's with the other. "This is our son. He's one year old."

"Hi. What's your name?" Val asked. The boy looked five and was fascinated with the lab equipment. He turned from one counter of test tubes and mysterious devices to another.

"Wayne. What's yours?" he answered, meeting Val's eyes.

She didn't need to see his karyotype. He had intense, intelligent eyes like Peter's.

"Is this your lab, Dr. Smythe? Can you show me around?" Wayne asked.

"I'm sorry I can't. This is Dr. Klein's lab. But you can ask him," Val said.

"Wayne, that's enough," Becky said. "These people don't have time for your questions."

Walt said, "Wayne, perhaps I can show you around later. But right now, I'm going to stick your arm to get a sample of your blood. It might hurt just a little."

Walt took some measurements, then said abruptly, "That's it. I think we'll be able to give you some answers soon. We appreciate your coming in. And thank you, Wayne, for being so cooperative."

"What about the lab tour?"

"Next time. I'll be calling your parents soon."

After they left, Val said, "He's a polyploid."

"Yes, there's not much doubt about that. I can hardly wait to see his chromosomes. A polyploid borne of diploids. Imagine the papers we're going to write about this!"

XXYY

Father Landry filled the doorway to Val's office.

"Come in, Father," she said.

Though his black cassock disguised the full measure of his corpulence, Val was still impressed by his size. If a polyploid was measured by girth not height, Father Landry would have been a candidate. Val motioned him to a straight-backed chair, wondering if the chair could handle his weight.

"Before you start, Father, I should warn you that I'm not going to argue with you about the humanity of polyploids. I think we know each other's positions."

"No, heaven's no. I only want to ask you about the epidemic of unusual children who are now a year old. This is all highly irregular. I'm sure you'll agree with me about that."

"Very well. And?"

"And these one-year-old children look much older, four or five years old, I'd say. And I hear from some of the parents that they're unusually precocious. Like polyploids. I believe you and your laboratory here at the university are testing these children. Is that right?"

"Yes, but we have no evidence that these children are polyploid. How could they be?" She lied, knowing she'd tell him nothing he wanted to know.

"I understand, Dr. Smythe, but let's suppose the children are polyploid. What I'd like to know is if there's a correlation between the flu virus and these young children. I believe there is."

"It's possible," she said.

"Anything is possible, Dr. Smythe. But hypothetically, help me out here, how could a virus cause polyploidy?"

She wished she'd read his columns more critically now. How much did he know?

"Generally speaking, retroviruses that cause influenza evolve through gene combination occurring within the organisms they've been attacking. In the organisms' guts. As a result, viruses are created with new protein coats and new genes. Our immune system is programmed to recognize the old protein coat but not the new one. So the new coat essentially cloaks the virus from recognition by our bodies. When our cells engulf the virus, its genes are released, and we get influenza symptoms. Contagion occurs when we pass the virus to other humans. So it's unlikely that has anything to do with polyploidy."

"But hypothetically, genes could be carried from polyploids to normal humans by viruses, is that right?"

"There is no known relationship between polyploidy and the influenza virus. We have no evidence to prove a connection."

"Then, Dr. Smythe. Let me ask another question. Do you think that the child I just saw in the parking lot, leaving from your lab with his parents is a polyploid? They're parishioners of my church."

He clearly enjoyed springing his trap.

"I'm sorry, Father. But I am not at liberty to discuss the private lives of any of the people helping us with our research. You know the laws. And I believe, correct me if I'm wrong, that you are also bound by another set of privacy laws."

"Fine. That's fine, Dr. Smythe. I'll know soon enough. I asked them to let me know about the karyotype results." Landry rose from his chair, clearly feeling he had won this little battle.

"Oh, by the way, Father. How are those Thailand trips of yours?"

Landry's face turned a purple hue as he shuffled out without answering.

Val walked down the hall to Walt's lab where she found him preparing the child's blood sample. He looked up, as she said angrily, "Father Landry came to see me. It seems polyploidy has diverted the church's attention from pedophilia."

"Forget him. He thinks he's found a gold mine. You can't stop ruthless people. At least not on your own."

"OK. So where are we? The virus would have to pick up a gene or genes controlling polyploidy, but polyploidy isn't carried by genes. Presumably. Dr. Solven used an herbicide to double chromosome numbers in fertilized ova. We can be relatively certain that the symptoms, rapid growth in the womb and early birth, were coincident with parents contracting the flu prior to conception."

"Sure. But we don't know anything for certain. Yet. Let's wait for the results, OK?"

XXXX

Val left work early in the afternoon to drive to Polysomia with David.

"I had an awful meeting with Father Landry this morning. If I believed in such a thing, I'd say he was evil," Val said.

"Yeah. Remember, I told you that I knew him when I was a priest. Is he still heavy?" David said.

"*Heavy* is an understatement. Can you imagine how much he has to eat to maintain his tonnage? I wouldn't want to be his shoes."

"He tended to be fanatical when I knew him but couldn't find a soapbox big enough." They both laughed, their humor easing some of the tension. "With the polyploid issue he's found a cause that will boost him up the church hierarchy."

"What's the story on Thailand, David? That's an odd choice of vacation spots for a priest. Does he go there on mission trips?"

"What I know about his trips are from Cici Lopez. She came to me for ID work so that she could keep her job as cleaner at the rectory. She'd lied to Father Landry about her citizenship status, and he was pressing her to prove she was a legal. One day when she was cleaning Landry's office, she discovered a bunch of DVDs hidden in a closet. She thought they were probably religious, and she was curious, so she borrowed one."

"Don't tell me they were porn from Thailand, David."

"Believe it or not. Cici returned the DVD to the closet, but when she did she noticed that there were fewer than before. Then one day he had a visitor that she recognized from pictures in the newspaper, President Dalhousie. She overheard them talking about the DVDs. Then when Dalhousie left, he had one in his hand."

"That hypocrite!" Val exclaimed.

"I thought you might find the information useful." He grinned at her.

They arrived at Polysomia to find the community bustling. Mary and Peter ran from the house to meet them.

"Grandma! Grandpa! I'm so glad to see you," Peter said. He wrapped his arms around Val, his red hair brushing her chin.

"You're taller every time I see you," Val said.

"Look, I have a new thumb. It grew back all by itself, but we didn't tell the doctors." Peter held out his thumb for inspection. Not even a scar of the original injury was visible.

"That's amazing, Peter. You're a special boy. I'm lucky you're my grandson."

"I gave everyone the flu, but I didn't get sick much. Just a little fever. Mommy says that's because I'm polyploid. Do you think that's the reason, Grandma Val?"

"Maybe so. You're a special boy in many ways," she said, knowing a hard life lay ahead of him. If only she could do something about it. Val turned and hugged Mary.

"You have a beautiful, extroverted child here. He must keep you entertained."

"He does that. With his own education and consultation about his teaching, he takes up most of my day. He's as eager to learn as I am. We have a formal discussion scheduled twice a week, but any time he wants to talk, we do. And that's a lot of the time."

"I can imagine," Val said.

"His students published an illustrated catalog of the species on the farm. Want to see it?" Mary said.

"His students?" Val said.

"The cafeteria workers want their kids to be like us. They asked us to teach them. Since then, friends of theirs have brought their children to be 'home schooled' too. I suggested that Peter help. And then he became one of their teachers. As you know, there's no better way to learn than by teaching."

"I have ten students, now, Grandma Val," Peter said. "I like being a teacher. We have lots of fun."

"Teaching is fun, Peter," Val said.

"Val wants to talk to Mommy about some things." Mary smiled at him. "Would you find your dad and help him with his work until it's time for dinner?"

"Sure."

"I'll go with Peter while you talk," David said.

Val and Mary went into the living room, and Val related her disturbing information.

"Mary, I think the governor will issue an order soon that says if polyploids are to stay in Louisiana at Polysomia, all females must have hysterectomies.

"I know, Val."

"You know?"

"We're pretty good at getting information, too. And we know they don't want us here. To them, we're aliens. Imagine how species from another planet would be treated if they landed on Earth. They won't leave us alone until we sign a treaty and submit to the operations."

"You're being awfully submissive, Mary. That's not like you."

"Sometimes we have to change to survive. And I want my child and the other children here to have the possibility of a good life. Living on a barren reservation far away from you and David and Grandpa and Grandma would be unbearable. You're my family."

Val felt like crying, and she was angry.

Mary said, "I have to talk to the others about this and see what they say, but I know they'll agree with me. There are five children among us now. Four of them are clones. None of the other couples want children, and no more parthenogenetic conceptions have occurred."

"That means you'll become extinct. I don't believe you want that to happen!"

"Maybe we're depressed. When others don't want you to exist, it's hard to make future plans."

"So what's next? Will you tell them? Do you want me to be there?"

"Yes, please. I'll call a meeting for tonight after dinner. Meanwhile, I want to show you my research on the possible variables controlling parthenogenetic conception. I've been working with Dr. Morton, the sociologist in your department. She helped me design the survey questionnaire, and I've been focusing on diets, relationships, things like that. We've surveyed polyploid females throughout the U.S. and compiled a database. My statistical analyses show that age and relationships are the most important factors. Of course, age is not a surprise, but I found that parthenogenesis never occurs in girls who have partners or who express the sentiment of being in love."

"Oxytocin!" Val almost shouted.

"I knew you'd say that." Mary laughed. "Of course, these results are only statistical, but they narrow the options for further study. Dr. Morton says I deserve a master's degree in sociology for my work. But I doubt that she'll be able to arrange it, considering the prejudice against us already."

A little later, they heard the dinner bell, and Mary stacked her papers neatly on her desk before leaving. They walked, hand in hand, the warm humid air enveloping them. From various directions, resident polyploids were following the scent of food to the cafeteria.

After dinner, at the community meeting, Val described the governor's plan. She expected questions but no one spoke. She sat down.

Mary stood and said, "What should we do?" No one spoke. "Then let me say, I expect the governor will order the National Guard to surprise us soon. As I see it, we can disperse and hide, try to fight them, or give ourselves up. If we run, we'll always be on the run. We'll be separated from each other, perhaps even our families. The National Guard is heavily armed, and we aren't. Fighting them would only lead to many people on both sides being hurt or killed. I for one will submit to the operation."

"This is blackmail, pure and simple," Paul said. "But you're right, Mary. We can't fight them, and if the girls don't submit, we'll have to run or live on a reservation. I say we take our chances here. But I'm just a man, so that's perhaps easier for me to say."

Martha stood next. "As you all know, I have a child conceived by parthenogenesis. I agree with Mary. Our children are destined to have to endure harassment and isolation just as we have."

She sat down.

"Thanks, Martha," Mary said.

No one else spoke.

Then Mary said, "OK. Each of you must decide what's best for you and your family. I care what each of you decides, so if you plan to leave, please let me know, and we'll help you any way we can. Are there any girls who choose not to submit to the operation?"

No one spoke.

"Then I guess we're all in this together."

CHAPTER 15

ather Landry arrived at the rectory in time for a pre-lunch snack before going to his office. His visit with Dr. Smythe had inspired a topic for his column, but he was worried about her mention of his visits to Thailand. He'd rewarded friends in high places and reassured himself that he was safe, protected.

He entitled his new column *The Wages of Sin*. Normal people were paying for the corporate sin of *in vitro* fertilizations that had culminated in the greatest evil yet: the creation of polyploids. The devil worked through science. There was nothing mysterious about that. Once polyploids were recognized, they had to be isolated, and the spread of polyploidy to normal people had to be prevented.

A yellow Post-It with a note in red ink caught his attention: *Call Governor Aucoin @ 337-988-4154.* How had he missed that? He reached for the phone.

"Hello, this is Father Landry from Vermilion. I'm returning a call from Governor Aucoin."

The governor came on the line in less than a minute. Father Landry again realized how important he had become.

"Yes, Governor, I'm aware of the urgent polyploid problem in Louisiana." … "No sir, I didn't know about Terrill and Smythe's insertion in the Senate bill" … "I agree, requiring hysterectomies is a fair trade-off for allowing them to remain in their community. I've advocated hysterectomies all along." … "Yes, I'd be honored to help you, sir."

Landry's thoughts drifted to how the governor's directive would change his sermon. His sheep must not lose focus.

"Good, you've handled the transportation with the National Guard." … "I'll contact my contact at the hospital and arrange a date for the operations."

Mary and her family were sitting in the cafeteria eating breakfast when they heard the trucks and buses arrive. She called Val, "They're here."

National Guard soldiers rushed into the cafeteria, pointing guns, as if they expected resistance.

"No one move!" one soldier yelled. "Remain seated and you won't get hurt! All females walk to the cafeteria door, single file, hands raised where we can see them."

Mary rose from her seat and leaned down to kiss Jon and Peter.

"Mommy, where are they taking you?" Peter asked, beginning to cry.

"Don't worry, sweetheart, I'll be back later. You can be with your daddy all day today instead of doing schoolwork. Won't that be fun? And I think you should cancel school for today."

"I guess so," Peter said sadly.

"Quiet! No talking!" shouted the soldier in charge.

As the girls filed through the cafeteria doors, the soldiers counted. "Get on the buses outside. The rest of you, stay in your seats."

Mary led the others to the back of the yellow school bus, past the driver in National Guard uniform. "Only one female per seat," the driver said repeatedly as they boarded. The buses smelled of the children who'd ridden to school in Arath that morning.

Five other soldiers with guns boarded the bus and spread out along the aisle. Many of the girls were crying. Mary and a few others tried to comfort them, until one of the soldiers shouted, "Everybody shut up! I don't want to hear any talking. Got it?"

Silently they rode the yellow buses to New Orleans. The irony of school buses being used for such a demeaning purpose didn't escape Mary's active mind. As she watched the Louisiana marsh land pass by, she tried to calculate how long the operations would take, how many doctors would operate, and how long it would be before she saw Jon and Peter.

The bus pulled into the emergency entrance driveway. All

except two of the armed soldiers got off the bus. These two pointed rifles toward the girls, and one shouted, "Get out, and don't make any trouble! Stay in single file behind that soldier. If anyone makes a wrong movie, you'll all be sorry." But the girls offered no resistance. Several of them were sobbing. Then, one by one, they disappeared into separate rooms.

A nurse said brusquely to Mary, "take off your clothes and put on this hospital gown. I'll be back to check on you in a minute." An armed guard remained in the room.

When the nurse returned, Mary asked her if the operation would be vaginal. "Yes. We want you out of here as soon as possible. You freaks."

XXYY

Mary opened her eyes in semi-darkness. She was in a hospital ward with curtains drawn between each bed. She felt sore inside. Val was standing in the darkness beside her.

"Mary, thank goodness you're awake. How are you feeling?"

"I've felt worse," she tried to joke. "When did you get here?"

"Jon called back to tell me that armed National Guard soldiers had loaded twenty of you on school buses," Val said.

"What about the others?"

"Everyone's OK. Jon said it all went peacefully. I think everyone was surprised. My guess is they would have used any excuse they could to shoot. You were right, Mary. This was the only way."

CHAPTER 16

Father Landry called the governor after breakfast. "Good morning, sir. I want to tell you about some new developments that concern the polyploids." … "Yes, that's great news about the hysterectomies. But this new development I refer to has been kept quiet until now. I intend to write a column about it today. But I wanted you to know ahead of time: There's an epidemic of polyploid children." … "Yes, normal people are having polyploid children. It has something to do with that outbreak of Polyploid Flu. The parents all had it." … "No sir, I don't know why no one has told you. The law binds doctors to protect the privacy of their patients." … "Yes." … "Yes, of course, it's premature to say that the children are polyploid before the results are known." … "Yes, I understand your predicament."

XXXX

Val was in her office when Dalhousie's secretary called to say he wanted to meet with her as soon as possible. She was reminded of Cici's story about Landry giving Dalhousie a pornographic DVD. Could she use that to help the polyploids? He had probably read Father Landry's column about the children of flu victims. But no one outside Val's lab group knew that Walt had found that Wayne, the Jordan's child, was polyploid.

"Dr. Smythe, have a seat," Dalhousie said, much too formally.

"Henri. I hope—"

But he interrupted. "Val, I'll cut right to the chase. I just heard from the governor. He's livid. As he put it, he's been caught flat-footed. He thought there would be no more polyploid births in Louisiana after the hysterectomies. But now normal people are having polyploid children. I want to know how these conceptions are connected to the Polyploid Flu."

"We've only examined one child," Val tried to explain. "Yes, he's polyploid, but—"

"Oh, my God, that's just what I was afraid of. I'll call the governor as soon as we're finished here."

Then he leaned back in his chair.

"We're going to have to have some changes here, Dr. Smythe. From now on, you will send any research results to me before they go anywhere else. And one more thing, the governor wants to make some changes in your department. He doesn't like its focus, and I don't either."

"What do you mean, the focus?"

"He wants people in the department who are more open-minded, that don't kowtow to the polyploid position. I'll give you some recommendations later. For one, we don't need that sociologist you hired."

"Is that all, sir?"

"Not quite, Val. The governor wants the university to change the name of your department to Polyploid Control. OK with you?"

As if she had a choice, she said, "Whatever you need to do."

As she rose from the chair to leave, the secretary rushed in. "Sorry to interrupt, sir, but Senator Emmett Terrill has been shot." She paused, took a breath. "And killed."

"Where?" Dalhousie said.

"In Vermilion, outside his home. Turn on your TV, sir. It's all over the news. He arrived from D.C. yesterday and planned to be home for a few days."

"This is very sad, but I'm not surprised. He's, I mean he *was*, entirely too bullheaded, staying on the wrong side of the polyploid issue. I told him so."

Val, shell-shocked, regained what little she could manage of her composure.

"Do you know Father Landry?" she asked Dalhousie, who was now staring at the TV.

"Vaguely, why?"

"I've heard that he brings gifts to his friends from Thailand. I thought perhaps you were one of those friends. It's strange that a priest would spend time in Thailand. Don't you think?"

Then she walked out.

XXYY

After lunch, Father Landry lumbered back to his office to check his messages. The governor had called and wanted to talk with him as soon as possible. As he savored his new importance, the governor rang back.

"Yes, sir. I'm fine. How are you? Is there a problem?" … "Did you say it's a polyploid? Well, that puts a new spin on the issue, doesn't it?" … "Yes. I'll be writing a column about this. I agree. People have a right to know."

The next call burst the bubble of importance the governor had puffed up. Dalhousie told him that Dr. Smythe knew about the gifts from Thailand.

"What a prying evil woman," Landry said angrily.

As he hung up he wondered. Did she also know about his gifts to his friend Jerry? Who had suggested the idea in the first place.

EPILOG

A Few Months Later

Mary sat at her desk thinking about the future of the polyploids. Since the mass hysterectomies in Louisiana, the polyploids had been emotionally devastated. Polyploids in other states had also been hunted down and similar treatments applied. It all seemed a huge mistake, a gigantic misunderstanding. Polyploids, if given a chance, could contribute much to the world. What should they do now? What could they hope for? What was the adult life span of a polyploid? No one knew.

Their fate resembled other extinctions. Diploids were intolerant or just plain xenophobic and eventually would rid the planet of all primates genetically similar to them. Neanderthals had lived side by side with diploid humans at one time and even interbred with them, and look what had happened to them. Other primates, no matter how distantly related, were being driven to extinction. At least polyploids had drawn attention away from internecine killings among diploids with only minor religious or skin color differences. But diploids wouldn't stop until all polyploids were dead. That had become perfectly clear. The sentiments of Hitler lay just under the skin of humankind, despite protests that such holocausts could never happen again.

Perhaps their community's money would run out, and extinction would be from starvation, not reproductive failure. The population of Polysomia had expanded considerably with inclusion of the new children who were now two years old. The government's promised allotment checks had never materialized, and a significant drop in the value of community investments, rising construction expenses, and the extra cost of caring for the new children had almost depleted Mary's financial assets from the sale of her father's Houston property. Although diploid parents had agreed to help, they had to be hounded monthly for their contributions.

Some polyploids had taken menial jobs on nearby farms. The acreage devoted to rice and crawfish farming provided enough support to keep the cafeteria operating. Perhaps they should consider conducting tours of Polysomia for a fee to see the freaks and how they lived, she mused, before realizing how desperate she sounded.

Mary's cell phone interrupted her thoughts. "Hello, this is Mary Solven." … "Detective Rodriguez? How can I help you? Is this about Michael?" … "Oh, it's personal? What do you need?" … "You want to bring me your child? But why? How is he different?" … "Oh, like us?"

The next morning Mary found a child sitting on her office doorstep. An unsigned note pinned to his shirt read: *Here's another one from Texas.*

"Hi, what's your name?" Mary asked. Judging from the child's wet shirt front, he had been crying.

"Simon," the child said.

"How long have you been sitting here, Simon?"

"Daddy drove all night. It was dark when he left me. Mommy stayed home. He said this was my new home."

Mary noticed a bruise on Simon's cheek and imagined that his clothing covered others. The child's tattered shirt was soiled with old food stains and probably hadn't been washed in weeks. His jeans were too small and as dirty as the shirt. He smelled strongly of urine, and his long, dark hair was tangled and matted.

"What's your last name, Simon?"

"Rodriguez."

"Ah. Are you hungry, Simon? The cafeteria opens for breakfast soon. But first, would you like a bath and some clean clothes? My son has some old ones that should fit you."

He smiled.

She took Simon to the farmhouse and introduced him to Peter and Jon who were just waking. Then she helped him bathe and washed his matted hair. As she'd suspected, his body was covered with bruises. The child delighted in her attention and put on Peter's jeans and T-shirt.

Then the breakfast bell sounded, and they walked to the cafeteria.

"I can show you around after breakfast," Peter said.

"I want to stay with Mary," Simon said.

"Of course, you do. We all do. But you can help me with chores in the meantime.

Then Mary said, "I'll find a book for you to take with you. Peter always finds time for his students to read."

"Oh no, I'm not allowed," Simon said, visibly shaken by the idea.

"But you're allowed to read here," Jon said. "Everyone reads here. We encourage it."

"But Daddy says reading at my age isn't normal."

XXXX

"Mary, two black SUVs are parked on the main road to Polysomia," Peter called from the porch.

"Are they National Guard?"

"I don't think so. They don't have any identification on the doors, but the license tags are U.S. Government," Peter said, his vision exceptional.

"It's starting again," Mary said. "We've got to find out who they are. And I know how we'll do it. The only place to eat around here is the Arath Café. Some of Grandpa's friends eat there. I'll call him to see if he can find out anything."

"Hi, Grandpa. It's Mary." ... "I think we might be in for more trouble. Several black SUVs are parked at the entrance to Polysomia. Have you seen them in town?" ... "Yes, thanks. Please let me know."

She put down the phone and said, "Peter, find your dad and tell everybody to stay indoors."

Mary watched as Peter ran toward a neighboring building where Jon had begun seeing patients in the clinic. Dr. Bradley had trained him, and now they worked side by side.

Mary continued to watch as more SUVs appeared. They were gathering forces, but why? Her phone rang, and Hank's voice came on the line.

"Grandpa, what? But we're not indoctrinating diploid children." ... "What ways? We're just trying to survive." ... "Father Landry?" ... "Thanks Grandpa. See you in a few minutes."

Armed people in uniform left the SUVs and marched toward Mary's office. She waited, wanting to talk to them. But one of the men raised a rifle and fired in her direction, deliberately missing. So she went back inside and called Val.

"Val, they've come for us. Grandpa says Father Landry and the FBI are working together." ... "Yes, I love you, too."

"We want everybody outside, immediately. You have three minutes." The voice came from loud speakers. "If you have any diploids with you, bring 'em out, too. We know you've captured some of our children."

Mary opened her office door and stepped outside into a misty rain. She looked toward the town circle. Dark clouds reflected back at her from the NanoSol coated roofs. Her friends were all standing outside now. Jon and Dr. Bradley stood in their blue physician's coats with their nurses and staff. Children huddled together.

As the men came closer, she could see their FBI badges. Mary counted eighteen.

Again the voice came over the loud speaker. "We're going to search every building here for hidden diploids and your perverted indoctrinating information. We know what you're up to. Do not resist. I repeat, do not resist. We have orders to kill. Senator Terrill isn't around to stop us this time."

And so it went, on and on. They searched through buildings, shouting, daring anyone to get in their way. But if there was an order to their search, Mary couldn't find it.

Eventually, seeming to tire of hauling away computers and other equipment in seeming randomness, their apparent leader said, "Are you Mary Solven?"

"Yes."

"Do you have any of our children here now? Do you ever have them here in this community?"

"Diploid parents sometimes bring their children for medical treatment. My husband and Dr. Bradford are very good doctors."

"Yeah, I'll bet. So, what else do you do to them?"

"I don't know what you mean. We don't *do* anything to them. We help with home schooling but only if we're asked. We teach them the same subjects you teach them in your schools."

"Why, you arrogant bitch. What makes you think *our* children need any help from your kind? Polyploids that parents bring to you belong here. But our children don't. All of this is your fault for spreading the Polyploid Flu to us." His face reddened. "How old are you, Mary?" He laughed as he said it. "I've heard how fast you all grow up and have sex and babies. But no babies anymore, huh? We fixed that didn't we?"

His face was close to hers now, and she felt spittle spray her cheeks.

"We mature faster than diploids. That's just the way we are."

"I said, how old are you?"

"Ten." Mary knew the number would anger him more.

"How can you be teaching our kids anything that is wholesome and Christian? You don't know anything. Where is this school where you teach?"

Mary pointed toward the modest one-room building they used for a school. The men marched off.

And so it went, on and on. Eventually, they'd leave, and then they'd be back. What was the point of it? Mary pondered. After all, eventually, they'd all be extinct anyway.

Why did humans continue to harass each other?

XXYY

The SUVs had gone now, and the residents of Polysomia had returned to work. For how long, they couldn't know. But they worked. They made the best of things. That was their purpose. To make the best of things. That, they believed.

And Mary sat, working as well, reconstructing their databases from carefully hidden back-up drives, when she heard Jon shouting from the street. He rushed into her office with a polyploid woman beside him.

"Tell her the news," he said. "Hurry."

The young woman smiled broadly and touched her stomach.

"I'm pregnant!"

www.ingramcontent.com/pod-product-compliance
Lightning Source LLC
Chambersburg PA
CBHW050747250626
47155CB00005B/1953